"You'll be perfect," Merry said, turning in her chair to face Buck. "I thought that the second I saw you."

He raised an eyebrow, obviously amused. "Oh, yeah?"

"Your blue eyes are killer. And a couple shots of you with your shirt off shoveling hay, well…" She suddenly realized that she'd said too much.

He smiled, knowingly. His blue eyes pinned her with a gaze so intense, she couldn't breathe. "So, you've been watching me, Miss Turner?"

His voice was throaty. Sexy. A shiver went through her.

"Well, not exactly." She tried to look anywhere but at him. "I was looking at you from a purely business standpoint."

"But you liked what you saw? From a purely business standpoint, that is."

"Yes. I mean no."

How *did* she get into this?

* * *

"Chris Wenger writes stories that tug at your heart and make you laugh out loud."
—*New York Times* and *USA TODAY*
bestselling author Carla Neggers

Dear Reader,

I am a native central New Yorker who has never left the area, but my sister moved to Tucson after she graduated from college. After one visit, I fell in love with all things cowboy, cactus and coyotes. Then I discovered rodeo, specifically bull riding. Yee-haw! Now my husband and I follow the Professional Bull Riders (PBR) and the Professional Rodeo Cowboy Association (PRCA). We've met many of the cowboys, bull fighters and stock contractors and have traveled to many events. These guys (and gals) are salt-of-the-earth types who come from hardworking ranch families. I've found that they are polite, honorable and truly good role models for their young fans.

That's why I love to write about cowboys. There's just something special about them.

So no matter where you live, get your favorite beverage, sit back, put your feet up and let me tell you about a cowboy who lives in Lizard Rock, Arizona, who meets his match in a TV star from Boston....

Cowboy up!

CHRIS WENGER

NOT YOUR AVERAGE COWBOY

CHRISTINE WENGER

Silhouette®

SPECIAL EDITION®

Published by Silhouette Books

America's Publisher of Contemporary Romance

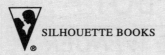

SILHOUETTE BOOKS

ISBN-13: 978-0-373-24788-2
ISBN-10:   0-373-24788-5

NOT YOUR AVERAGE COWBOY

Visit Silhouette Books at www.eHarlequin.com

Printed in U.S.A.

Books by Christine Wenger

Silhouette Special Edition

The Cowboy Way #1662
Not Your Average Cowboy #1788

CHRISTINE WENGER

has worked in the criminal justice field for more years than she cares to remember. She has a master's degree in probation and parole studies and sociology from Fordham University, but the knowledge gained from such studies certainly has not prepared her for what she loves to do most—write romance! A native central New Yorker, she enjoys watching professional bull riding and rodeo with her favorite cowboy, her husband, Jim.

Chris would love to hear from readers. She can be reached by mail at P.O. Box 1212, Cicero, NY 13039 or through her Web site at christinewenger.com.

To the memory of my sister, Sue. How I miss you.
To my cowboy brother-in-law, Rick. Hang in there.
To Alex and Katie. Your mother will always
be in your heart and mine.

Chapter One

Where on earth am I?

Meredith Bingham Turner pulled her generic gray rental car over to the side of the road—what little side there was. Rolling down the window, she peered down the drop-off to her right and frowned at the scruffy vegetation and huge prickly cacti that stood with their arms raised toward the blazing Arizona sun.

It was hot. *Very hot.* And she was very, very lost.

Once again, she read the directions to the Rattlesnake Ranch that her friend Karen had e-mailed her, but something was still wrong, and there was no one around to ask for assistance. No cops. No pedestrians or joggers. No shoppers. No tourists.

Just lizards, scorpions and tarantulas.

She shuddered and quickly rolled up the window. She hadn't seen any of those creatures yet, but why tempt fate?

Two weeks ago, Karen had called Merry and asked for a favor. "I know you're busy, but it's important. My brother is at his wit's end. With Caitlin's psychiatrist bills, Louise's and Ty's tuition and all... Well, we might just lose the ranch if we don't do something drastic. Besides, I read about you and that George fellow in *Celebrity Gossiper,* and it sounds like you need a break, too."

Karen was right. She needed to get away from Boston and her corporation. She needed to get away from George Lynch, her latest "kiss and tell" ex-boyfriend. Whenever she thought of the headline in the *Celebrity Gossiper:* "Sensational Cook Not So Sensational in Bed," she wanted to scream.

Merry did the only thing that she could do. She turned it over to her lawyers.

"Of course I'll help," Merry had replied to Karen's request. "What do you need me to do?"

"Help us turn the Rattlesnake Ranch into a dude ranch. I can take care of the business end, but I'll need decorating help, menu-planning, maybe you could help with publicity. An endorsement by you would guarantee a full house."

"I'm coming up with ideas already," Merry replied.

She was more than happy to help Karen. Karen had gone out of her way to help Meredith, a lonely introvert from Beacon Hill in Boston, loosen up at Johnson and Wales University. Those four years at

J&W with Karen as her roommate had been the best time of her life.

Karen was her only friend in the world. She could trust Karen with her innermost thoughts, feelings and problems and know they wouldn't end up in the *Gossiper.*

Maybe it wouldn't be too awful here in the desert. All she had to do was to come up with some decorating ideas, lend her name to garner some publicity for the launch of the dude ranch, and then she'd fly back home to Boston and her beautiful condo overlooking Boston Harbor.

Karen believed there was a market for "wannabe cowboys," especially from the Northeast. Merry supposed that there were some city slickers who wanted to play cowboy for a week and go on trail rides and chuck wagon cookouts, even though it didn't sound like fun to her. Why would they travel all the way to Arizona? Then again, corporations liked that kind of thing for team building. Maybe that was the answer—attract the corporate crowd.

Whatever Karen wanted, Merry would roll up her sleeves and do anything she could to help.

Merry studied the map that the auto club had marked out for her and thought that she had to be somewhere on the little gray line between Dead Man Mountain and Galloping Horse Mountain.

Wild West names were just so colorful, but she wasn't in the mood for colorful names. She needed better directions.

She looked out of her rearview mirror. Not a car or a person in sight. Not a soul to ask how to get to

Hanging Tree Junction—another colorful name. It would have been nice if someone had thrown up a sign at frequent intervals, so she would at least know if she was still in the United States and not in Mexico.

Maybe she should just keep going forward. The sun would be setting soon, and she didn't relish driving on twisting and turning mountain roads in the dark.

And then she saw him.

Her first real-life cowboy.

He was moseying, as they say, toward her, riding a big black horse. The cowboy wore a long white duster. Only a bit of faded denim was visible under his brown leather chaps with black fringe. As he rode closer, she saw that he had silver spurs on his boots.

She couldn't take her eyes off him. He looked so rugged, at one with the landscape. So did the rifle butt sticking out of a long leather rectangle hanging from his saddle.

Rifle?

Her mouth went dry and she braced herself, ready to floor the gas pedal.

The cowboy squinted into the sun. She couldn't make out the color of his eyes, but she'd bet the next royalty check from her latest cookbook that they were as blue as the sky above.

If she lived to talk about it, she'd have Joanne, her new publicist and assistant, hire him for the video shoot advertising Karen's dude ranch. He'd be perfect.

He tweaked the front brim of his white cowboy hat in casual cowboy fashion as he approached, and she melted—even though the air conditioner was on full blast.

His horse stopped at the side of her car and proceeded to wipe its nose on her window.

Thank goodness it was a rental car and not her Jag.

He motioned for her to roll down the gooey window.
With her foot poised over the gas pedal, she hit the
button with her left hand and opened the window a few
inches. She stared up at the cowboy, and wished she
could see more of his face. The horse was tall and, so
it seemed, was he. She craned her neck, keeping a wary
eye on horse and rider.

"Howdy, ma'am." He did the hat-tugging thing
again. "You lost?"

"Undoubtedly."

"I take it that means yes."

"Yes."

"Would you be Meredith Something Turner?"

She raised an eyebrow. "I'm Meredith *Bingham*
Turner."

"Close enough."

"And you are?"

He pushed his hat back. "Bucklin Floyd Porter. But
people call me Buck."

"You're Karen's brother!" Thank goodness. She recognized him now. She remembered seeing pictures of
Buck and Karen's other siblings whenever Karen
returned to college from visits home. She'd always
thought he was handsome, but the pictures didn't do
him justice—especially when he was in full cowboy
regalia.

He nodded. "And you're the lady who's going to
help turn my home into a dude ranch?"

She put the window down completely and leaned farther out. "That's me."

He shook his head, not seeming happy at all. "If you don't mind, I don't want to stand around talking in this heat. Karen sent me to fetch you."

"Fetch? As in dog?"

"Fetch as in she knew you'd get lost. She said you'd need road signs every couple of feet."

So much for the strong, silent cowboy. "Glad you're here. Lead the way."

She could see his eyes twinkling in amusement. They were blue. Sky-blue, just like she knew they'd be.

"You can't follow me, ma'am. I'm headed down there." He pointed at a path through the cacti. "I'd strongly suggest that you stick to the road."

He turned the big black horse and began to give her directions, pointing and waving his hand down the road. She stuck her head farther out the window to hear what he was saying over the blasting air-conditioning. As she did, his horse swung its tail, stinging her in the face.

"Yeow," she yelled, pressing her hand against her burning cheek. She leaned back into the car as the horse pranced beside her.

The beast swung its tail again. This time she was spitting the horse's tail hair out of her mouth and brushing it away from her eyes. Her elbow hit the horn.

The horse whinnied, took off at a gallop, leaped the guardrail and plunged down the cliff with Buck Porter hanging on for dear life.

* * *

"Whoa, Bandit. Easy boy."

Buck pulled on the reins, but not too much. He might as well give Bandit his head and just go with it. The Bandit could handle anything.

Why the hell had the fool woman laid on her horn? Didn't she know that it would spook his horse?

Buck leaned as far back in the saddle as he could. Cactus needles stabbed into his duster and scraped his chaps. During the plunge down the mountain, it didn't take long to figure out that Meredith Something Turner was going to be trouble.

"She's a celebrity chef. She's on TV and has written several cookbooks," Karen had told him. "She'll bring in a lot of good publicity. Besides, she's my best friend, and I haven't seen her in a long time. We can do some catching up."

Buck didn't want any part of turning Rattlesnake Ranch into a dude ranch. He liked it just the way it was. Unfortunately, he didn't have much choice. He'd been outvoted by his two sisters and brother, who, along with him, each owned one-fourth of the Rattlesnake, left to them by their parents.

"Whoa, Bandit," he yelled, leaning back even more. "Easy, big guy."

Finally, Bandit hit level ground and stopped dead in his tracks. Shaking his head, the big black stallion pawed at the ground with a hoof.

"Yeah, I know. I know. The city gal probably didn't know any better."

He heard a sound like the wailing of a coyote and looked up. There she was, hanging over the guardrail.

"Do you need help?" she yelled.

She'd made a megaphone over her mouth with her hands. If he did need help, what would she do? Make blueberry scones?

"No," he shouted back.

"Are you hurt?"

She was scaring every bird, animal and lizard within a fifty-mile radius. Bandit was fidgeting like he was going to jump out of his skin.

"I'm fine," he yelled. "Get in your car and go."

"But I don't know where to go."

"Go back to Boston," he mumbled, then shouted, "Follow the road until the end. Turn left, then right, then your second left. Rattlesnake Ranch will be on the right."

"Any of these streets have colorful Western names? You know, something I can remember?"

"Like Beacon Hill?" he said.

"Wha-a-at?"

"No. No names." No one ever bothered naming the dusty paths that ran through Rattlesnake Ranch, least of all him.

"Right. Left, left. Then turn right. Or did you say two rights? I should write this down. Right? Stay there until I get a pen and paper from my purse, will you?"

Oh, for Pete's sake. He had chores to do, and leading a city gal around by the nose wasn't one of them.

A scream cut through the air, startling the buzzards and vultures right out of the trees. Her again.

He released his grip from the saddle horn and catapulted off Bandit. Grabbing his rifle and rope, he ascended the same path he'd just ridden down.

"Meredith? Hey, Meredith Something Turner, are you okay?"

Silence.

"Answer me, dammit," he shouted, struggling up the steep incline.

The gravel crumbled under his feet, but he was making progress. Cactus needles stabbed his arms through his duster, through his shirt. Sweat poured down his face as he scrambled higher...higher.

He set the rifle down, shook loose some rope, twirled it over his head several times and let it fly. It hit his target—a post of the guardrail. He tugged to test it and took up the slack. With his rifle tucked under his arm, he climbed up the rope hand over hand as quickly as he could.

"Meredith?"

Another scream split the air.

In one smooth motion, Buck vaulted over the guardrail, rolled to the ground and took aim....

What the hell?

Two wild burros were eating the contents of Meredith Something Turner's purse. Papers and cosmetics were spread out on the road, and the burros were busy grazing on them. She was pressed against her car, wide-eyed as another burro nibbled on the lapel of her pink suit.

He could tell she was ready to let loose another granddaddy of a scream, and he didn't think his ears could take any more.

But she surprised him. Instead of screaming, she

croaked out, "Don't shoot them. Just get them away from me."

He lowered his head, so she wouldn't see his grin. Securing his rifle, he got up from the ground and took off his hat.

"Shoo," he said, waving the air with his hat as he walked across the road. "Scat. Go on. Get on. You're scaring the lady and she's scaring half the state of Arizona."

They eyed him, then trotted off down the road.

Buck turned toward her. "What the hell's wrong with you? You scared me half to death."

"You? You were scared? What about me?" She walked over to the mess on the road, picked up a pack of tissues and, after careful inspection, blew her nose into one. "What were those things?"

"Wild burros."

"W-why aren't they in a zoo?"

"This isn't Boston, lady."

She sniffed and brushed off her lapels. "No kidding."

Bending back down, she picked up her purse and began to toss items in it. "My purse has a hoof print on it. They chewed on my cell phone. And they ate my makeup." She stopped to looked at him. "There are stores around here, aren't there?"

Buck didn't think she needed any makeup. In spite of how she irritated him, he had to admit that she was one of the prettiest women he'd ever seen. And he didn't know much about fashion, but that pink suit she had on looked expensive. So did her gold jewelry.

Everything about the woman looked expensive.

He sure hoped she didn't expect to be waited on. Karen wasn't feeling well, and he had a ranch to run. In his experience, women who were on Meredith Bingham Turner's level were too high-maintenance.

"Yeah, we have stores around here. We have a feed store over in Lizard Rock. Oh, and there's a John Deere store in Cactus Flats, too."

She stared up at him with big green eyes, probably trying to figure out if she could get makeup shipped from Boston via overnight mail. Then she glanced down the road at the burros, which had stopped to graze. "You will stand guard, won't you? In case they come back."

He choked back a laugh. "Yeah, I'll stand guard."

"Thank you." She sniffed. "But don't shoot them."

"No, ma'am."

She bent over to pick up more items from the road, and he couldn't help noticing how the fabric of her skirt molded against her perfect butt.

"Mr. Porter, where is your horse?" She stood straight and focused her eyes on his rifle. "You didn't have to shoot it, did you?"

"Lady, I don't shoot everything that moves out here. If I did I'd have to carry all my ammo on a packhorse," he snapped, then realized she was dead serious. She'd probably seen too many westerns on TV where animals were put down. Remembering she was from Boston, he softened his voice. "Bandit's fine. He's probably back in his stall and eating dinner by now."

"Bandit?"

"My horse."

"How are you going to get home?"

"I thought I'd ride with you."

"You cowboys ride in cars?"

She really was a slicker, unless she was pulling his leg, as he'd pulled hers. He couldn't tell.

"I'll give it a try."

Speaking of legs, hers were blue-ribbon winners. Her hair was the color of corn silk and probably just as smooth to touch.

What the hell was wrong with him? He was waxing as romantic as a cowboy poet. If he didn't stop himself, he might break into song and start yodeling.

She had to go. She was going to be nothing but trouble. He could feel it right down to his bones.

But one thing he knew for sure, he wasn't going to spend half his born days bailing a tenderfoot like Meredith Turner out of trouble. He had a ranch to run.

Or what was left of it.

"Would you like to drive, Mr. Porter? You do know how to drive a car, do you not?" She held out a key with a yellow paper tag hanging from it. Her voice held a bit of sarcasm. She was pulling his leg.

He slapped his thigh and added a dumb grin. "Gee, shucks, ma'am. Ya mean I can drive a real car like this?" He went over the top with a Texas accent. "How about if I drive you back to the airport? This place isn't for you."

She was silent for a dozen heartbeats, and Buck immediately regretted his words. He was being a knothead. If Meredith was as big of a celebrity as Karen said she was, the new Rattlesnake Dude Ranch would be a success.

He supposed he should be happy about the plans for the ranch. It would be the answer to his financial problems, but he just needed more time to come up with the money himself. He had a plan, but the clock was ticking and the bank foreclosure was looming.

His plan was to sell the furniture he'd been making. An old Army buddy owned a fancy gallery in Scottsdale and had scheduled a show and sale for him. Whether or not his sale would be a success was a crapshoot, but he was keeping his fingers crossed.

Meredith met his gaze. "Your sister said she needed me. Therefore, I intend on helping her in any way I can. So if you don't want to drive, point me in the right direction and I'll find my own way."

Loyalty. Buck admired that, but he still didn't want a bunch of dudes on the ranch he loved, wandering around, playing cowboy and sleeping and eating inside his parents' house. He had Caitlin to think of, too. His daughter had retreated so deep into her own world since her mother left that he just couldn't reach her. A bunch of strangers might make her withdraw even more.

His siblings disagreed, particularly Karen. She felt that Cait needed people around her, especially kids her own age to encourage her to open up more. He reluctantly agreed to give it a try. He'd cut off his arms if it'd help his daughter.

He tried to point out that even if the ranch did turn a profit, it wouldn't be that significant. The ranch was in the red almost two hundred thousand bucks, give or take, and the bank said he had to pay that off before he could borrow another penny to diversify into stock contracting for rodeos.

He wished he had the money to buy them all out, but that was spitting in the wind.

He let his eyes skim over the generous curves of his sister's friend. Maybe it wouldn't be all that bad having her at the ranch. If nothing else, she was fun to tease and easy on the eyes. He could use some fun in his life.

Cait seemed to be looking forward to Meredith's visit, or at least that's what Karen assumed. Every Tuesday when Meredith's cooking show was on, Karen would microwave some popcorn and the two of them would watch it together.

He should be used to Cait's silence toward him by now, but he wasn't. He kept hoping that someday she'd say something—anything. He wanted to hear his little girl's voice again, to hear her call him Daddy.

Meredith Something Turner tossed him the keys and mumbled a question about whether or not Lizard Rock or Hanging Tree Junction, Arizona had a dry cleaner.

He was willing to bet she wouldn't last a week here before he'd be driving her back to the airport and his home would be safe from change.

Then he hoped like hell that people would like his furniture and buy it. If they did, he could get out of the red a lot faster and his home would still be safe.

But by then it might not be his.

Chapter Two

Buck skillfully guided the rental car down the narrow mountain road, but Meredith still found herself holding her breath on every twist and turn. The craggy rocks were so close to the car, she could reach out and touch them. Every fallen tree branch looked like a snake or a lizard, and every other stone or twig was either a tarantula or a scorpion.

Swallowing hard, she adjusted the air-conditioning vents until the cold air blew right on her face. As she took a couple of gulps of the air, she decided that she was being ridiculous by scaring herself like a teenager at a summer camp bonfire.

But still, there was no sign of civilization as far as she could see. No hotels. No stores. No banks. No fast food places. Arizona was as foreign to her as Jupiter.

She stole a glance at Buck. He was so tall that he had to take his hat off to sit in the car. His hair was jet-black and tied back in a ponytail with a piece of leather. It made him look more masculine than some of the men back home with their neat Boston haircuts.

Merry remembered the day that Karen had called her, sobbing about Caitlin, and how devastated her brother was when his wife had walked out. Apparently, Buck's wife, Debbie, had left for Nashville to pursue a singing career more than two years ago, and Cait had stopped talking from that moment on. Buck was having a hard time dealing with his daughter's silence.

Buck had found a psychiatrist for the child to see, but based on Karen's last call, the little girl was still withdrawn and still not talking to anyone.

Merry stole another glance at Buck. How awful for him to have gone through so much pain. In a way, he'd lost his wife and his little girl on that same day two years ago. Karen had said that he'd barely left the barn for a year or so, and was there all hours of the day and night, barely sleeping.

His siblings, Karen, Louise and Ty, had told Buck he needed to snap out of his funk, for his daughter's sake. He finally had, and tried to make things up to Cait, but she still wouldn't talk.

Sighing, Merry concentrated on remembering the road, the road that would take her back to the airport when she was done with her business here. But there were no landmarks, no side streets and still no signs. They just kept climbing, twisting, then descending.

Buck must have heard her sigh. "It's not much longer," he said. "About twenty more minutes."

"Thank you." She racked her brain for more conversation, but for a woman who made a good chunk of her income as a TV personality, she couldn't think of a thing to say to this man with broad shoulders and dark stubble that made him look more than a little dangerous.

The weather was always a safe subject, so she dove in. "Have you had much rain lately?"

"It's the desert."

"Oh…I guess not, then." So much for conversation with the cowboy. She twisted her fingers together and checked her manicure, remembering how Karen had gotten her to stop biting her nails. Seeing her good friend again would be wonderful.

She looked out the window. Every so often, she was surprised by the flash of color from a patch of fragile-looking wildflowers, or daunted by a lethal-looking cactus, both co-existing in a strange type of harmony.

All right, so this wasn't Boston. It was…tolerable. And she told herself that there weren't acres of poisonous reptiles out to get her, just wild burros.

She resolved to concentrate on helping Karen just like she'd promised. The sooner she did that, the sooner she'd be back home in familiar territory.

With that decided, she relaxed her grip on what was left of her purse.

"Over there." Buck pointed off in the distance, to his left. "Rattlesnake Ranch."

She craned her neck and squinted. "Where?"

"Over there."

"Over there" got closer, then disappeared again, as they turned another bend and descended until the mountain road turned into packed dirt barely wide enough for a car. They were on flat land now, up close and personal with the desert.

Buck turned right and before them was a bleached sign proclaiming Rattlesnake Ranch. She shuddered involuntarily and immediately her eyes scanned the road for anything slithering.

"Um…Buck?"

"Yeah?"

"About snakes…"

"What about them?"

"Do you have a lot of them out here?"

His blue eyes glanced at her briefly, and then returned to the road. "It's the desert."

"Of course there are snakes" was what he didn't say.

Quit obsessing, she told herself.

They rolled to a stop in front of a sprawling ranch house.

"Here we are," he said.

Merry heard the obvious pride in his voice. She took out a notebook and leafed through it for a clean page, free from burro slime, and found a pen at the bottom of her purse. Brainstorming time had arrived.

At first sight, the ranch house was welcoming. Designed in traditional Santa Fe architecture, it had a big porch that ran the length of the house. Bright flowers spilled out of terra-cotta pots of every size and shape along the brick walkway. More colorful flowers cascaded from hanging baskets.

Beautiful.

She knew that the flowers were Karen's doing. She'd always had a green thumb and went into the business program and floral arranging curriculum at Johnson & Wales with the hope of opening her own florist shop.

The car door opened, startling her. Buck held out a hand to help her out, and she placed her hand in his. She wasn't a small woman, but when his rough, callused hand covered hers, she felt very feminine and protected.

She tried to analyze why she was having a cowboy fantasy, when a small hurricane descended down the thick wood stairs.

"Merry! It's been so long."

Buck dropped her hand, and Merry found herself in Karen's bear hug.

"I see my lug of a brother found you, or did you find him?"

Merry laughed. "He found me. I was lost."

"I knew it," Karen said, turning toward her brother. "Buck, thank goodness you're okay. When Bandit came home without you, I got worried and sent Juan and Frank out looking for you. What happened?"

"It's a long story," Buck said, carrying Merry's suitcases up the stairs, as easily as if they contained feathers instead of a closet's worth of clothes.

Merry scribbled in her notebook. That would make a perfect picture for Karen's brochure—a rough-and-rugged cowboy bringing luggage up the stairs of the dude ranch.

Perfect.

Buck stopped on the porch and looked down. "Karen, where do you want this stuff?"

"In your bedroom, Buck."

He raised an eyebrow.

"Well, you haven't been using it," Karen snapped, and then turned her attention back to Merry.

At just the thought that she'd be staying in Buck's room and sleeping in his bed, Merry's heart flip-flopped in her chest, and her face heated as if she were a teenager. *Jet lag. It must be jet lag. Or the low elevation.*

Karen gave her another hug. "I am so glad to see you in person. I watch you on TV all the time, but it's not the same."

"It's good to see you, too." And it really was.

"How's business?" Karen asked.

"Overwhelming." She'd hired an additional publicist, Joanne Gladding, to handle the George Lynch fallout. Joanne was a go-getter, but Merry wasn't sure that Joanne was right for her. She'd hired her anyway, though, because she was leaving on this trip, and the matter had to be deflected immediately.

Whenever Merry thought of the tabloid articles, a new layer of humiliation settled like lead in her chest. Her parents were still absolutely furious with her about the one before George Lynch—her assistant director Mick, who also blabbed to the tabloids about their relationship.

Her parents. They never missed an opportunity to remind her not to get involved with an "underling" ever again, saying that her actions reflected on them and their business, too.

She never could win with them. Yet something inside her still made her want to keep trying.

Merry pushed her parents and the George Lynch fiasco to the back of her mind. She was going to enjoy her time here.

"I have some presents for you from Boston and Rhode Island." Merry opened the trunk of the car and began to lift out some boxes. "I hope everything made it in good shape."

She handed Karen a couple of the boxes. "This is chocolate-covered fruit from that shop by City Hall, and this one contains those cookies we lived on in college. And I bought some homemade bagels from Mrs. Jeeter, who said to say hello to you. And...ta-da...some New England clam chowder, packed in dry ice, fresh this morning from Clamdiggers."

"Be still my heart." Karen laughed. "But no clam cakes from Rhode Island?"

Merry pulled out a bright purple bag. "Two dozen of them right from Point Judith."

"You're a sweetheart."

Singing the song they'd made up about Johnson & Wales University, their alma mater, they climbed the stairs and entered the ranch house.

Merry stood on the thick, glazed Mexican tiles and looked at the brightly striped serapes over the couches and side chairs, the rough-hewn beams, the beehive fireplace in the corner and the thick wood furniture. She could smell fresh paint.

"Karen, it's beautiful. The pictures you sent didn't do it justice. The architecture is magnificent. It's so homey."

Peeking out from behind one of the couches was a small, blond-haired girl with big blue eyes—just like

Buck's. She had two straight ponytails that started high on her head and brushed her thin shoulders.

Caitlin. Merry gave a cheery wave and a wink to the little girl, who then disappeared back behind the couch.

Merry raised an eyebrow at Karen.

"Cait, come and meet my good friend Meredith Turner," Karen said. "You know her. We watch her on TV all the time."

But there was no sign of Cait again.

Karen turned to Merry and shrugged. "She just loves to watch *Making Merry with Merry* with me. She even helped me make your chocolate-chip snowball cookies last Christmas."

"Maybe we can make them together, even though it's not Christmastime. I like them all through the year." Merry felt as if she was doing the dialogue from her show.

Merry deposited her tote bag on the gleaming plank floor and looked around again. "It's perfect, Karen. Your guests could gather here and play cards, or read a book by the fire, or just talk."

"I can't wait," Buck said sarcastically, walking into the room.

"Buck, for heaven's sake, Merry is trying to help us." Karen lifted her hands in the air, as if she were giving up.

"And to that end, I was thinking of a feature on my show once the ranch opens, like a 'before and after' segment. I can get a crew out here, and they can start filming the 'before' segment."

"Think of the publicity. It'd be fabulous." Karen clasped her hands together.

"You'll also need a brochure and a commercial. We might as well take care of both of those, too." Merry leafed through her notebook. "I have some ideas."

"Excellent," Karen said. "I knew you'd help."

Merry eyed Buck. He seemed less than thrilled. Matter of fact, his face looked like he had just eaten something sour. "Karen, you were the business major, you have to tell me your ideas."

"Let's have some chowder and clam cakes first." She looked into the bags and pulled out plastic containers. "Then we can talk business."

"It's a deal, but I'd like to change first, if you don't mind," Merry said. "Some burros thought my suit was lunch."

"I can't wait to hear that story." Karen laughed and raised a shopping bag in the direction of a hallway. "Last door on the right. I'll show you."

"Don't bother. I'm fine. You go and find a place for all the goodies."

"Don't be long," Karen said. "I can't wait to catch up."

Merry felt a warm feeling building inside and spreading out. She hadn't felt that in a long time. Real friends were hard to find, and Karen was a real friend.

Merry inched down the hall to the bedroom, stopping at frequent intervals to admire the bold paintings of cowboys and cowgirls at work. She hoped to catch another glimpse of Caitlin somewhere.

"Would you like to join us, Buck?" Merry heard Karen say.

"No, thanks. I'd rather muck the stalls," he answered. Then the door slammed.

She flicked the light on in Buck's bedroom. She had to brace herself against the sheer force of masculinity. It was a man's room with its big, thick furniture and no frills. Her gaze focused on the centerpiece of the room, a bed that looked as if it had been shaped from a fallen tree.

Merry was instantly drawn to the bed. She inspected every inch of it, and reminded herself to ask Karen who the artist was that had created such a masterpiece. For heaven's sake, it looked as if there were some buds ready to bloom on some of the branches that were twisted to form the headboard. More branches formed a canopy above. It was almost as if the wood were still alive.

She imagined lying on the bed as green leaves and flowers cascaded above.

Exquisite.

A vivid blanket in blocks of stripes and arrow designs covered the bed, and she couldn't resist inspecting the workmanship. It was handmade, and unless she missed her guess, it was the genuine Native American article.

She noticed a huge bleached-wood armoire that was the focal point of one wall. A matching seven-foot-long dresser lined another, and on each side of the bed were matching nightstands accented with saguaro cacti ribs in the doors. She had seen similar pieces in galleries in New York City and Boston, but nothing as magnificent as these.

Against another wall was a couch, but on closer inspection, she saw it was actually a futon or a daybed. The arms were of thick wood with inserts of some kind of long, spindly, bleached wood on the back for ornamentation. Lying on one of the colorful cushions of the futon was a beat-up, floppy stuffed cat. She assumed it was Caitlin's.

Merry picked up the pathetic beige cat with only one eye, and remembered a similar cat. Hers. She'd called it Bonita, and she had been a Christmas gift from Pamela, their housekeeper and cook, because her parents wouldn't let her have the real thing, no matter how much she begged or no matter how good she was.

Merry had cried many times into Bonita's gray fur. Once, she remembered coming home to find Bonita missing. She looked all over the house, sobbing. Finally, her mother had ordered her to stop crying and told her she was too old to play with a stuffed cat.

Merry had been inconsolable. She knew in her heart that her mother had thrown Bonita away. The cat had become too dirty and too worn to be a resident of the Beacon Hill house any longer.

She returned the cat to its exact place and chuckled as she remembered how she'd rescued Bonita from the trash can in the alleyway in the dead of night.

She'd hid Bonita from her parents from then on. Currently, her childhood confidant, lovingly mended and with additional stuffing, rested on an antique rocking chair in the bedroom of her condo.

She looked at all of the various cowboy and Indian artifacts that were displayed in the room. Each piece was a work of art and seemed to be positioned perfectly.

If all the guestrooms looked like this, and with the media blitz that Merry had planned, the phone would soon be ringing off the hook with people making reservations for the Rattlesnake Dude Ranch.

Gingerly, she sat down at the edge of the bed, and bent back to study the twisted canopy of branches over her head. She imagined Buck lounging on the bed, wearing nothing but his hat, holding out his hand for her to join him there.

Suddenly feeling warm and jittery, she jumped up and walked over to the huge windows lining the three walls. She could see the corral and the barn and the setting sun, which was just about to disappear in a blaze of orange and yellow behind the craggy mountain that seemed close enough to touch.

She noticed Caitlin pressed against the barn, covertly watching her father brush Bandit. Buck must have spotted the girl because he set the horse's brush on a post, and walked over toward Caitlin, smiling. But instead of staying to talk to him, she ran away.

Through the open window, she could hear him call to her. "Caitlin. Cait." She could hear the anguish in his voice, see him shake his head and kick the dirt with a booted foot.

The girl was running fast, down past the barn, until she vanished behind another outbuilding.

He turned back to Bandit. As he petted the horse's neck, she heard the deep rich tones of Buck's voice. Although she couldn't make out his words, Bandit nodded as if he understood what Buck was saying to him.

She'd always heard that a cowboy's horse was his best friend. Now she believed it.

As she was about to get ready, she saw Karen blazing a quick trail to Buck. Angry words floated on the air, and Merry wondered what they were fighting about, not that it was any of her business. She knew that Karen was close to all her siblings, and they shared exactly what was on their minds. That was one of the things that Merry had always envied, the fact that Karen had a large, close family and they all cared for one another.

An only child, Merry had been nothing but lonely.

As if Buck and Karen sensed her presence, they both turned and stared. Startled, she backed away from the window, but not before she saw Buck shake his head and Karen cover her mouth with her hand as they noticed her watching them.

With a sinking feeling, she turned away, opened her suitcase and changed into a pair of expensive new jeans she'd just bought, and a peach blouse that felt silky against her skin.

Karen would tease her unmercifully when she saw her in designer ranch clothes. Merry smiled. She hadn't been teased in a long time, and she needed it.

A gray cloud intruded on her light mood as she thought of the scene she'd just witnessed between brother and sister. She already knew that Buck didn't particularly want her here, but why? Surely, he wanted the Rattlesnake Ranch to generate a big profit. Didn't he?

Well, that was the reason she was here. It would be an added bonus if she could get a little rest and relaxation. She needed it desperately. And maybe she could think about how to get a handle on her own business.

It was getting too hard to manage with all the culinary products she'd been venturing into—pots and pan, a line of spices, stainless steel utensils, synthetic bakeware and heaven knows what else.

It seemed that lately everyone wanted a piece of her.

Merry let her hand glide over the exquisite bureau one more time and glanced over her shoulder at the incredible tree bed. Then she closed the door behind her and went to find Karen.

She needed to know what was going on before she decided whether or not to unpack.

Chapter Three

Merry leaned against the rounded archway to the kitchen and studied her friend. "So tell me what progress you've made on the dude ranch idea, and tell me what's going on with your brother, not necessarily in that order."

"I never could keep anything from you." Karen smiled as she set plates, mugs and bowls on a thick pine table.

Merry walked over to the table, picked up a plate and studied the artwork. A sketch of a cowboy galloping his horse and roping a calf was centered in the middle. Under the drawing were two *R*s back-to-back with a wavy line under them.

"That's our brand," Karen said. "And that's my

father roping that steer. My mother drew it and had the plates made years ago."

Merry thought about the time and trouble Karen's mother had expended to make such a personal gift that meant something to the whole family. It was in stark contrast to the very expensive, very bland, English bone china with the gold-leaf border of the Turner family.

"You know, Karen, I think that if you get mugs made up in this pattern, your guests would buy them for souvenirs. Have you thought of a gift shop? It would be perfect in a corner of the lobby—I mean the living room."

Karen ladled clam chowder into bowls and the steamy soup scented the air. "Before we discuss the dude ranch, I have something to tell you."

Merry noticed that her friend's face was somber. Whatever she was going to say wasn't good news. Merry put the plate down, pulled out a chair and sat down.

"I just took a call from my doctor. I have to have my gallbladder out in three days."

Merry reached for her friend's hand and squeezed it. "I didn't know you were having trouble. You never said anything."

Karen took a deep breath. "It's all so sudden—the surgery, I mean. But I've been having pain for a long time now. And it's getting worse. It was selfish of me not to call you and tell you to postpone your trip, but I wanted you here. I couldn't leave the ranch in such a state of flux, especially when we're hoping to have our first guests in a few months. I didn't want to call Louise. Her bar exam is this week and—"

Merry took a deep breath. Already her brain was listing things she needed to do. Where was her notebook?

"Leave your sister where she is, and don't worry about a thing. Meredith Bingham Turner, the Goddess of Hospitality, is on the scene," she said with more confidence than she felt. "How long will you be in the hospital? Are you having laser surgery?" Merry knew that laser surgery had a quicker recovery time.

"No such luck. They have to take it out the old-fashioned way. They think I'll have to stay in the hospital about four or five days."

Merry bit back her disappointment. She'd been looking forward to spending a lot of time with Karen, just like the old days when they were living at the dorm.

Well, she could still have the long talks. Merry would just have to visit Karen in the hospital.

"There's something else." Karen grimaced as tears shimmered in her eyes.

Merry prayed that Karen wouldn't tell her that she had more health problems.

"It's nothing too serious." Karen opened one of the boxes that contained a Boston cream pie. "I need a favor, and I know it's an awful imposition, especially when you told me over the phone that you were burned out and needed a break after all that horrible publicity about you and…and what's his name?"

"George Lynch, but forget about him. My good friend needs me. I can take care of things on the home front."

"Thanks. I knew you would." Karen smiled weakly.

"But there's Caitlin. She needs someone to watch over her. Buck is so busy with the cattle and all."

A door opened to the mudroom off the kitchen, and Merry recognized the white duster and white hat through the glass-topped door. Buck. She heard the sound of something hitting the floor—his boots.

Karen's eyes darted to her brother, and she stood. "How about some coffee, Buck? I was just about to make some for Merry and me."

"Sit down, sis. I can get it."

Suddenly, Karen gasped and doubled over. Buck hurried to her side, holding her so she wouldn't fall.

"I can't take it anymore." Karen puffed out the words, grimacing in pain.

Merry rushed to her other side. "What can I do?"

Buck thrust out his chin in the direction of the phone on the wall. "Call 911 and get an ambulance here. Then get a hold of Doc Goodwater."

She barely had time to nod before Karen gasped again. Buck swept Karen off her feet and held her. She groaned into his chest.

"The doc's number is tacked to the bulletin board on the side of the phone," Buck advised. "Let him know Karen's on her way to the hospital. Tell him that her surgery has just been moved up."

Merry hurried toward the phone. Buck left the kitchen, still with Karen in his arms. She could hear them talking in the living room.

When the 911 operator asked Merry the location, she realized that she had no idea where she was. She could only say "Rattlesnake Ranch."

"Buck Turner's place?" the operator replied. "What's wrong?"

Thank goodness for small towns. "Gallbladder. Karen."

"An ambulance is on the way."

"Thank you."

Merry punched in the doctor's number and left a message with his service.

Then she poured Karen a glass of water and hurried into the living room with it.

Karen was curled up on the couch with some pillows under her head. Buck sat on the edge of the couch and held on to his sister's hand.

"What about the ambulance?" Buck asked her.

"It's on the way."

"Thank you." His deep voice was rich with emotion when he spoke those two little words. Gratitude showed in his eyes, and it was obvious that he was glad she was there to assist him. That made Merry warm right down to her toes.

"The pain is gone," Karen said. "I'm okay now. I can last until the operation."

No," Buck said. "This has gone on long enough."

Karen winked at Merry. "If I were a sick horse, he would have put me out of my misery a long time ago."

She took a sharp breath and closed her eyes, and the slow stream of a tear traced a path to her ear. Her pain was back.

Merry turned to look for a box of tissues, but just as she did, Buck reached over and wiped his sister's tear with his thumb.

Merry's heart melted as she wondered yet again what it would have been like to have siblings. Would they have been as close as the Porters?

She heard the distant wailing of the ambulance. Buck must have heard it, too. His blue eyes looked up at her, and he sighed in relief.

"Buck, I'd like Merry to come with me in the ambulance. Would you mind?"

"Whatever you want, sis. This is your show. I'll follow in the pickup with Caitlin." He looked around. "Where's she hiding now?" His voice held a hint of frustration.

"Caitlin," he shouted, but the little girl didn't appear.

"Buck, why don't you stay here at the ranch with Cait?" Karen asked with a strained smile. "You know how you get around anything medical."

"I want to make sure that you're okay," he said.

Karen shook her head. "Are you sure I can't convince you to stay put? Caitlin will probably be up too late."

"She doesn't have school tomorrow. Besides, Merry needs a ride back, unless you want her to stay at the hospital all night with you."

"No. Of course not."

"Then it's settled. I'll get my boots." He walked over to the mudroom. "Caitlin," he shouted again. "I need to talk to you."

When Buck left the room, Merry took his place on the couch and held on to Karen's hand.

"Cait has been doing well in her special ed class," Karen said softly. "Her teachers are wonderful."

Merry nodded. "That's great."

Karen closed her eyes and winced from more pain. "Underneath all his bluster, my brother's a pussycat."

"Since you're in the middle of a gallbladder attack, I'll excuse that misfire."

"You'll find out for yourself soon enough." Karen chuckled, then grimaced in pain. "But maybe I shouldn't leave you two here alone for five days. I could become an aunt again in nine months."

Merry's cheeks heated. "I don't think there's a snowball's chance in the desert that anything like that is going to happen between us. We clash."

Karen's hand closed tight around Merry's. "Take care of Buck and Cait while I'm gone," she said, her voice barely more than a whisper. Her hand relaxed, her eyes closed, and her head sunk deeper into the pillow. "They've been having a real tough time."

Two long hours later, in the waiting room of the Lizard Rock Hospital's emergency room, a doctor dressed in aqua-colored scrubs caught Buck's eye and motioned for Buck to follow him into a small conference room. In turn, Buck gestured for Merry and Cait to follow. Buck introduced Doctor Goodwater to Merry as Karen's visiting friend.

"And, Doctor, I think you remember my daughter, Caitlin."

The doctor tweaked Cait's nose, and she quickly retreated to stand in a corner of the room, clutching her stuffed cat.

"Buck, we're getting Karen ready for surgery," the

doctor said. "She's scheduled for eleven in the morning." He checked his clipboard. "She's in room 4014—you can go see her now."

"Thanks, Doc." Buck pumped the doctor's hand. "Take good care of her."

"You know I will."

They took the elevator to the fourth floor and found Karen's room easily. Karen was already hooked up to IVs and seemed to be dozy, but was fighting it.

Caitlin headed for a chair and sat wedged into the seat as far as she possibly could, still clutching her stuffed cat.

Merry's heart went out to the girl. She seemed so detached from everything and everyone. It was as if she was in her own little world and didn't welcome intruders.

Merry went over and stood before her, not daring to touch her. "Your aunt Karen is going to be fine, Caitlin. Don't worry."

Cait never made eye contact. She curled up into an even tighter ball and buried her face in the stuffed cat.

Merry had an overwhelming need to somehow break through to the girl. In a way, Merry had been just as withdrawn and shy when she was Cait's age, but Merry had been starved for someone to talk to, someone who'd pay her attention to break through her shyness. Cait didn't seem to care.

Merry had heard the old chestnut, "Children should be seen, but not heard," a million times from one of her parents, usually whenever a dinner guest would comment on what a well-behaved child they had. In

Merry's case, she was just trying to be perfect to please her parents. Cait had more significant problems.

What could she do to reach Caitlin that her family and the best psychiatrists couldn't? Merry was a TV cook and a hospitality expert. What made her think that she could break through Cait's shell?

Merry petted the stuffed cat's head. "What's your kitty's name, Cait?"

Silence. Merry looked at Karen.

"Tell Merry that your kitty's name is Princess, Cait," Karen said.

Cait remained silent, so Merry decided to tell her a story. "Princess. What a perfect name for your pretty kitty. My kitty's name is Bonita. I've had Bonita since I was a little girl. Do you want to know a secret, Cait?" Merry could see a hint of interest in the girl's eyes. She lowered her voice to a whisper. "I told Bonita all my secrets. I bet you tell all yours to Princess."

Merry could have sworn that Cait gave a slight nod. She didn't know if she did that regularly or not, but it made Merry feel good.

She turned to Buck to see if he'd noticed Cait's small reaction to her. He gave a slight nod and a wink indicating that he had. For some reason, that made her feel even better.

"Buck?" Karen motioned for Buck to come over to her bedside. She put her hands around his neck as if she were choking him, and said, "Get out of here, you big lummox, so I can get some sleep."

When he bent over her bed, she hugged him. "Really, Buck. Take Merry and Cait home. Merry's dead on her feet, Cait is tired and so are you. There's nothing either of you can do here."

"I'll call Louise and tell her what happened," Buck said. "And then I'll try to find Ty. One of his buddies will know which jail he's in this time."

Karen yawned. "He's up at the line shack and you know it. And make sure Lou doesn't come home. She needs to take her bar exam."

"She'd better pass so she can get a job and finally earn her own keep. I'm not supporting her any longer." His voice was gruff, but his eyes twinkled.

The ride back to the ranch was quiet. Cait slept sandwiched between Merry and Buck. Even in sleep, she was guarded. Her head didn't lean any farther to the left, because if it did, it would have rested on her father's arm. Nor did she lean to the right, as Merry was there, a stranger she only knew from TV.

Merry wanted to know what had happened between Buck and his daughter to make the little girl shun his affection. Could Cait still be that traumatized because her mother had left her? Maybe it was because Buck had thrown himself into his work and ignored her at a critical time in her young life.

Merry supposed it was possible that both of these things could have made Cait withdraw.

It was obvious that Buck loved his daughter, but he seemed frustrated as to what to do at this point.

Out of the corner of her eye, she saw Buck gently take Cait's little hand and hold it. Merry blinked back tears. At least when the girl was sleeping, she didn't pull away from him.

Merry's own eyes wouldn't stay open, and she felt herself floating into sleep. Her head was so heavy, she couldn't help but lean the side of her face against the cold pane of the truck's window.

She let herself drift off, just a little.

"Hey, Meredith Something Turner, wake up," whispered a deep voice. "We're here."

"This isn't Boston," she mumbled, trying to get the cobwebs out of her brain.

"Far from it."

Rubbing her eyes, she noticed that the passenger's side door was open, and Buck held his daughter and the stuffed cat—Princess—in his arms.

Then she remembered. She was at the Porter ranch.

She scrambled out of the tall pickup, shut the door and followed unsteadily behind him, more than a little sleep-drunk.

"Would you mind opening the door? The key's under the third flowerpot from the right."

Merry found the key and was unlocking the door when she heard Buck humming a soft tune. She stole a glance at the big cowboy, swaying slowly, studying his daughter, who was sleeping peacefully in his arms.

By the light of the moon, she could see the love on his face. Yet bone-deep sadness was visible in the tightness around his mouth. His daughter couldn't—*or wouldn't*—return his love.

He met her gaze as she held the door open for him to enter the house.

When he was halfway down the hallway with Cait in his arms, he asked, "Is there anything you need?"

"No. I'm fine. You just take care of Cait."

He shifted his daughter's weight. Cait gave a little sound but never woke. "Cait has been sleeping in here because her room is being painted. We were going to move her to Karen's room when you arrived, but her room isn't done yet, either. The painters just need one more day so they can finish up. Then we can get everything back to normal." He hesitated. "I don't know what Karen had in mind for sleeping arrangements for Cait tonight. The two of them were sharing my bed. Every other room is cluttered with furniture and smelling of paint. I could put Cait on the couch in the living room."

"Don't you dare put her on the couch. If anyone goes on the couch, it'll be me. Cait can have the tree bed." She remembered that Buck had moved out of his room. "I could take the futon, that's perfectly fine with me. But I don't want Cait waking up, seeing me, and being scared. I'm really a stranger to her."

"*Everyone's* a stranger to her," he whispered.

Merry followed Buck into her room. She flung back the linens of the tree bed. "She must be getting heavy."

"Never."

He set his daughter down gently, her head on the pillow. He took off her shoes and set them on the floor. Then he placed the stuffed cat next to her. He moved the sheet, blanket and comforter over Cait and gently brushed her hair from her face. He kissed her softly on the forehead. "G'night, Caitie. May your dreams be as sweet as you."

How beautiful, Merry thought. *How loving.* If just once her mother or father had said something like that to her, but they never had. She'd gotten all her kind words from Pamela, the housekeeper.

He stood, looking at his daughter for a while, and then turned as if suddenly remembering that Merry was there.

"I should get you settled." He looked around the room. "Where did Karen put the linens for the futon? They're probably in the closet in the bathroom."

He suddenly looked tired.

"I can handle it."

He nodded. "Thanks."

"Buck, are you sure I shouldn't sleep on the couch? If she wakes up and I'm here—"

"Hard to tell what Cait will do. She seems to tolerate you more than some," he said. "She knows you from TV, so you're not a complete stranger. I'm sure she'll be okay, but it's late, so if you don't mind for one night…"

"No. Not at all."

For what seemed like an eternity, he stared at Merry. "You know, if you're scared to be alone, I can sleep here, too."

She raised an eyebrow.

"I meant that I'll take the couch in the living room," he added, and grinned. "But really, there's nothing to be afraid of. There hasn't been a snake or a burro in the house in…" He looked at his watch. "In at least two hours. But let me get my rifle, and I'll have a look under the futon for you."

Terror struck deep into her bones. Snakes? But even

in the dim light, she saw the twinkle in his eyes, and she knew she was being teased.

"Buck, you don't have to sleep on the couch. You can go to the...um..." She couldn't think of the word that Karen had used earlier. "Barracks?"

"Bunkhouse."

"Yes. Go ahead. We'll be all right."

He tweaked the brim of his hat and walked out of the room. In the doorway, he paused and looked back. "Thanks again...for everything," he said, but didn't leave. "Um...Cait might have a nightmare. I just wanted you to be aware of that."

With that, he was gone.

A nightmare. Terrific.

She could make an eight-course meal for a party of fifty. She could decorate a three-thousand-room hotel and casino. She could write bestselling cookbooks, change the Porter's home into a successful dude ranch like they'd asked her to do, but she knew nothing about children.

Meredith Turner had never been a child herself.

The windows of the room stared back at her like huge, blank eyes. She undressed in the bathroom.

Even though Buck had been teasing her about snakes, she hated to have her fears thrown in her face. She hated to show one chink in her armor. Her competitors would like nothing better than to find something on her, something past or present that they could zero in on.

She was supposed to be the perfect woman, the perfect hostess, the perfect cook and homemaker.

Meredith Bingham Turner, Miss Hospitality.

If she believed her own hype, there wasn't anything she couldn't do. ·

She found a sheet, blanket and pillow in the linen closet in the bathroom, and began to make up the futon.

Listening to Caitlin's gentle breathing, she wondered again what demons had a hold of the sweet little girl.

Merry knew about demons. She was a personal failure, in spite of her business success. Men wooed her, then they used her for her clout or for her bank account, or both, so it was impossible to know whom she could trust.

She couldn't get a compliment from her parents even if she received every award known to humankind. She needed to get better control over her company, and she needed a break from men. Her one true friend was in the hospital, and Merry had a gut feeling that Bucklin Floyd Porter and his daughter were going to test her mettle.

So no matter how handsome he was, no matter how delicious he looked in jeans, no matter how sweet he was to his daughter or how his deep voice made her think of moonlit nights and satin sheets, the last thing she needed was to get involved with him or Cait.

Then again, he hadn't asked her to get involved. She was just here to do a job. And that was a good thing because she had nothing else to give anyone.

Chapter Four

Buck shook out the folded serape and picked out a couple of pillows that were positioned on the furniture.

He'd decided to sleep on the couch after all, just in case Cait had her usual nightmare. He wanted to be nearby. Karen usually handled nightmare detail, since his presence sometimes made things worse, but Meredith shouldn't have to deal with it.

He also didn't blame her if she didn't exactly feel safe. After all, she was a city girl who didn't know her way around a ranch or the desert.

With her big green eyes, shiny blond hair and designer everything, Meredith was a tenderfoot and totally out of her element. It wouldn't be long before she was gone, and that was fine with him. Although he appreciated her help with Karen's illness, and her attempt to be nice to Cait, he didn't want her changing his ranch—his life—around.

Until he could put her back on a plane and get the time to work on his furniture—his plan to save the ranch from bankruptcy—he'd keep an eye on her, for his sister's sake.

He supposed he owed Merry a debt of gratitude for coming to help. It wasn't her fault that the ranch was going under. He'd tried like hell, but he couldn't turn a profit. There had been too many unforeseen expenses after his parents had died. Because he'd wanted his brother and sisters to go to college, he did what he had to. He refinanced and took out loans. Because he wanted Caitlin to go to the best psychiatrists around, he took out more loans.

At this point in time, the Rattlesnake Ranch needed to diversify and not depend only on cattle. He'd hit the area banks and applied for more loans so he could buy a couple of bulls with a good track record that he could breed to some of his more outstanding cows. He also wanted to buy a half-dozen good bucking horses and some basic breeding equipment that he needed to get started. All his applications were denied. Bank after bank told him that he had too big of a debt load already.

Karen, Louise and Ty had insisted that something serious had to be done. Hell, Buck always thought that, too, which was why he wanted to get into rodeo-stock contracting.

Then Karen suggested the dude ranch thing, saying that the profits could go into paying off all the loans first. Then he could develop the rodeo-stock part of the operation.

That might happen if he lived long enough, but it wouldn't happen in the year that he said he'd give them to make the dude ranch a success.

Already he couldn't stand the thought of strangers living in his house. The ranch meant everything to him, much more than it did to his brother and sisters. Karen wanted her own nursery and flower shop in town. Louise had set her sights on being a corporate lawyer. Ty—well, Ty didn't know what he wanted yet, but he definitely didn't want to be stuck on the Rattlesnake much longer. Ty liked to roam.

Buck wanted to buy them out, and he was pretty sure they'd all want to sell. They just didn't have the love of the land that he had. He knew that they were only sticking around because they felt that they owed him.

But they didn't owe him anything. After the car accident in Florida that killed his parents, he just did what he had to do, plain and simple, and was glad to do it.

He'd been in the Army and assigned to Fort Benning, Georgia, when he was called into the chaplain's office and told that his parents had died. It had been his folks who'd encouraged him to take some time off from the ranch and see the world after he graduated, and when the Army recruiter came to his high school, he'd thought it was the perfect answer. He could see the world and serve his country while doing so. Mostly, though, all he ended up seeing was Fort Benning for a year as an assistant to the captain of Human Resources.

He'd received a hardship discharge from the Army and came home to take care of his brother and two sisters, even sending them all to college, just like his folks would have wanted. Now, to save the ranch, he'd had to go along with his siblings. He hated to do it, but his gallery sale wasn't scheduled until six months down the road. He'd tried to stall things until then but was overruled, and the wheels started moving even before Karen had placed that call to Meredith. His sisters and Ty didn't want to wait until the sale.

"Why bet against a sure thing?" Karen had asked.

The Rattlesnake Ranch was going to become the Rattlesnake Dude Ranch, and Buck was powerless to halt things at this point.

Porters had ranched this land since after the Civil War. He'd die before he sold to that lunatic Russ Pardee, who made him periodic lowball offers. Pardee probably already knew that a Southwest developer, the Jace Corporation, was interested in making a golf course and condos for the rich out of a chunk of the Rattlesnake, and he no doubt planned to turn Buck's land over to them for a fat profit.

In the dim light, Buck scanned the family room. Everything in it held special memories for him. He remembered his mother painting all the pictures that were displayed. There was Ty riding his first horse. Louise, with her red hair flying, running barrels. Buck, his dad and Gramps fishing by the river. Karen potting flowers.

He remembered helping his dad put in the beehive fireplace around which the family gathered every night.

Blankets, rugs and pottery made by their Pima Indian friends were displayed through the house.

He had to give Karen a lot of credit for playing the Meredith Turner trump card. He should be grateful that there was a way out, but he was going to be the laughing stock of Arizona when he opened his ranch to dudes. Russ Pardee would see to that.

Damn. His brain was going in circles. He wanted to get rid of Meredith so the dang-blasted dude ranch wouldn't be a success, but that would be like kicking himself in the ass.

He needed to shut down and get some sleep, but he was finding that harder and harder to do with everything on his mind.

Now he had Karen to worry about. He wondered how his sister was doing over at the hospital. She'd looked so sick and pale. He knew she'd be okay after her surgery, but he hated for her to have to suffer all that pain. He said a quick prayer for her, tried to get comfortable on the couch, closed his eyes and hoped that sleep would come.

Merry awoke to the neighing of horses instead of the sound of honking traffic. She couldn't remember where she was, but twisted tree branches were over her head.

Burrowed into her side on the bed was a little girl with light blond hair. Caitlin.

Cait had had a bad dream during the night, just as Buck had said she might. She'd been crying and whimpering in her sleep, and Merry remembered getting up and putting her arms around her. Then she'd lain down next to Cait in the tree bed.

Merry had pushed back Cait's sweat-soaked hair, and in the girl's sleepy state, she'd mumbled, "Mommy, why don't you love me?"

Merry felt the tears stinging her own eyes. She remembered thinking the same thing when she was Cait's age.

After Cait was quiet, Merry got up to go back to the futon. Then the girl had said, "Mommy, don't go."

Merry looked at the sleeping child. She had Buck's jaw and maybe his nose. She definitely didn't have his thick black hair. She wondered about Debbie, Buck's wife. There weren't any pictures of her in the house, and Karen hardly spoke of her.

Merry decided to get up and start breakfast. Carefully, she moved away from Cait so as not to wake her.

On her way to the kitchen, Merry stopped, startled by the sound of soft snoring. As her eyes adjusted to the light, she saw the massive form of Buck sleeping on the couch in the living room. His chest was bare and broad with just a hint of black hair. A blanket was draped— *barely*—across his middle and over one leg, but his other leg was exposed from his thigh on down.

Her fingers itched to touch the hard muscles of his chest and arms. She wanted to trace a path with the palm of her hand down his tight stomach and let it linger. Instead, she tucked her hands into the satin-lined pockets of her khaki pants and forced herself to steady her breathing, then she hurried to the kitchen.

The kitchen had *always* been her sanctuary.

She paused for a minute as she flipped on the light switch, wondering why Buck was intruding on her waking moments as well as her dreams.

It was more than a little unsettling to be so attracted to Buck. He wasn't her type at all.

But who was her type? George and his kiss-and-telling to the tabloids had hurt her to the core. Before George, it'd been her assistant director, Mick.

Mick had charmed her in the hope that she'd make him director. After she'd given him her heart and soul, she'd come close to doing just that. Luckily, or unluckily, she'd caught him in a lip-lock with the studio's receptionist.

She'd finally learned her lesson with George. She was going to be more careful than ever. In fact, she might forget about romance altogether.

Merry pushed all that to the back of her mind and flipped the switch to start the coffeemaker. She admired the bright Mexican tiles, and wondered if Karen's mother had a hand in designing those, too. It was a great kitchen with yards of counter space and gleaming appliances.

Everything about the rambling ranch house was homey and comfortable. It had the feel of a close-knit loving family.

It was a shame to turn it into a dude ranch. This was a house meant for a family. Oh, sure, guests would feel warm and welcome, but the house wouldn't speak to them like it spoke to her. It represented everything she'd never had growing up.

Cranking open the windows above the sink, she took in a deep breath of the cool morning air. Instead of the smell of Boston Harbor, Arizona had the scent of horses and something else…mesquite maybe, or sage.

Morning was her favorite time of the day. She loved to sit with a cup of coffee and watch as the world around her came to life.

She noticed that distant mountains looked like a lacy silhouette against the orange glow of the sky. At the base was a smoky layer of clouds that made the mountains look like they were floating. She knew that it was going to be hot soon.

As Buck kept reminding her, it was the desert.

The chirping of the birds surprised her. Back home, the squawking of the seagulls drowned out any other birds that might be nearby, but here in the desert, the birds were singing in several-part harmonies. It was all a glorious cacophony of sound, and right now it sounded better to her than the Boston Symphony.

She peeked into the refrigerator, looking forward to the prospect of cooking a big breakfast for Buck and Cait and maybe even the ranch hands. Instead of the pressure of testing recipes for her show and making sure everything was just perfect, she could cook for the fun of it, just like she had once upon a time. Before cooking became her gold mine, then her albatross.

As her eyes skimmed the contents of the refrigerator, her mind quickly sorted everything into various combinations of dishes. She could make several different quiches, or omelets, or even her ham-and-cheese scones.

Depending on when everyone usually ate, she might even have time to make her maple biscuits.

She wondered what Buck would want for breakfast. She figured him for the meat-and-potatoes type, nothing fancy, so he'd probably like eggs like rubber and bread that was carbonized. He'd want potatoes swimming in grease and onions and a hunk of artery-clogging meat. She could do that.

She glanced in the direction of the living room where Buck slept and wondered what, if anything, he had on under that blanket. She wanted another peak at him lying on the couch.

As if by magic, the door opened and Buck materialized. "G'morning." He rubbed his closed eyes with the tips of his fingers. "I checked on Cait. She's still sleeping."

He ran his hands over his chest as if he was rubbing himself awake, and Merry couldn't turn her eyes away. He wore only jeans, but a white, long-sleeved shirt hung around his neck, the same shirt he'd been wearing last night. He clearly wasn't a morning person in the least, but he looked very male, from the top of his disheveled black hair to the bottom of his bare feet.

He yawned, then sniffed the air, his eyes still at half mast. "Coffee?"

"It's not quite ready yet," Merry answered. "Can I make you breakfast?"

The second his eyes focused on her, he froze and blurted, "I thought you were Karen."

"Hospital."

"Right."

"How about breakfast?"

"Uh, no. I have to take care of the horses." He crossed the room, bent over to grab his boots, then he hurried out the door.

Looking out the window, she saw Buck hopping as he pulled on his boots. He shrugged into his shirt and continued walking as he buttoned it. He let out a low whistle, and several horses that were in the corral moved toward the fence and hung their heads over it. Laughing, he petted their noses.

"I overslept, ladies and gents, but I'll feed you now," she heard him say.

The coffeemaker gave a final chug, and she decided to deliver Buck's coffee to him at the barn and watch him feed the horses. Since she didn't know how he took his coffee, she found a silver tray, draped a yellow-checked napkin over it, and set a creamer and sugar bowl on it along with a spoon and two mugs of coffee, one for him and one for her.

Tentatively, she walked out to the corral, ever alert for anything that crawled or slithered. She could feel every pebble under her feet, and knew for a fact that she should have packed some sturdy shoes rather than strappy Italian sandals.

He was tossing hay with a pitchfork when he saw her coming. She held out the tray, and he smiled as he took one of the mugs. She smiled back.

"Just black. Thanks. You're a lifesaver." Taking a long draw, he swallowed, then grimaced and coughed. "What did you do to this?"

"Nothing. I didn't do anything to it."

"It tastes like…hell, I don't know."

"Vanilla?"

He stared into the coffee as if a cockroach was doing the backstroke in it. "I guess so."

"That's because it *is* vanilla."

"That's not coffee," he growled.

She chuckled. He was cute when he was cranky. "My mistake." Of course, Buck wouldn't like flavored coffee. What had she been thinking?

"I'm sorry. I just like my coffee to taste like gun cleaner."

She turned to leave. "I'll make another pot."

"No. Don't bother. I'll get some in the bunkhouse. The boys always have a pot on."

"I'll be glad to get it for you, but Cait—"

"I'll know if Cait's up," Buck pulled out a radiolike object out of his pocket, clicked it on and hit a couple of more buttons. "Intercom." He handed her his mug and pointed in the direction of a long, low, gray shack. "Cookie has been dying to meet you."

Cookie turned out to be a gnarled, white-haired, bow-legged cowboy with the most terrific bright green eyes she'd ever seen.

He took off a battered black hat from his head and clutched it to his chest. "Meredith Bingham Turner. It's you. In the flesh. Why, you're even prettier in person than you are on *Making Merry with Merry*."

"You watch me on TV?" Never would she expect that a tough-looking cowboy like Cookie would watch her TV show.

"I never miss it. I've adapted your cinnamon coffee cake recipe for baking in a Dutch oven over a campfire. The cowboys love it. Well, all except for—"

"Buck."

"Yeah."

"Speaking of Buck, I came for some gun-cleaner coffee for him."

Cookie nodded. "I'll get it for you. Come in. I didn't mean to leave you out here on the porch while I yammer."

Merry followed him into the bunkhouse. It was surprisingly neat and tidy with several twin beds lined up around the room on the right side. On the left was a well-stocked kitchen and a long wooden table with bench seats. "I smell—"

"Bananas," Cookie supplied. "I was going to make your tropical French toast in honor of your arrival, but now that you're here, as one cook to another, can I impose on you to—"

He looked at her so adoringly, she couldn't resist.

"I'd love to make my French toast for you, Cookie. How many will I be cooking for?"

"Eight, if Buck joins us."

"And then there's Cait, if she ever wakes up," Merry said.

The time went by fast as she and Cookie worked side by side. He was a knowledgeable assistant. The cowboys filed in as if on cue, all smiling as they began heaping their plates. She could barely keep up with the demand or the compliments, but all she knew was that it was just wonderful cooking for such an appreciative audience.

"What's going on here, boys?"

Buck stood in the doorway with Caitlin at his side. Merry had forgotten about bringing him his coffee.

He looked at his ranch hands. "Don't you boys have work to do?"

Half standing, they swallowed some last bites and hurried out the door, giving him a wide berth.

"Miss Turner, I won't have you bothering my hands or disrupting my ranch. They have work to do."

Merry shot him a cool look. "I was just cooking breakfast for them. It feels good to do something for someone who appreciates it."

"Meaning I don't appreciate what you are doing here?"

"Not that I can tell."

Cookie put his hands on his hips and stepped closer to Buck. "Listen here, you big galoot, it's not every day that the boys get breakfast prepared by the beautiful, famous Meredith Bingham Turner. And what made you grumpier than a bear this morning?" Cookie gave an exaggerated wink. "You didn't sleep here last night, so you should be nice and calm this morning."

"Not that it's any of your business, but I slept in the house."

Cookie looked from Meredith to Buck, then picked up a cast-iron frying pan and held it menacingly in the air.

Merry laughed. "Buck slept on the couch to be close to Cait."

He set the pan down and shook a gnarled finger at Buck. "You take care of Miss Merry, you hear, boy? Or you're going to have to answer to me."

"Yes, Marvin." Buck's eyes twinkled as he seemed to snap out of his bad mood and poured coffee into a battered metal cup.

"Don't you call me that, *Bucklin Floyd!*" The frying pan was back in Cookie's hand. "Now git. I have some

French toast to enjoy with Miss Merry here and Miss Caitlin." He leaned over to wink at Cait, but she raised an arm and tucked her face into her elbow.

"Cait already had some cereal, and they both have to get moving if they want to go to the hospital with me to visit Karen. Remember? Her operation's this morning."

Merry jumped up. "Of course I want to go. Let me get ready."

"Make it fifteen minutes. I want to take a shower in the bunkhouse first," Buck said. "Merry, would you take Cait with you?"

Merry nodded. "Of course."

Buck squatted to be level to talk with Cait, but the girl looked away. "Brush your hair. Okay, Caitie?"

Cait simply walked away and stood by the door, waiting.

"I'll help her," Merry said, doubting if the girl would let her. She gave Cookie a peck on the cheek. "We'll have to do this again."

Cookie blushed and grinned. "Someday, do you think you could make your maple biscuits? I've tried them, but to have them made by you would be a real treat for me and the boys."

"I'd love to."

Buck shook his head. "What's wrong with plain old biscuits?"

"These are like heaven," Cookie said. "Just wait until your dude-ranch guests get a taste of them. I'll be asking for a raise. Got that, Bucklin?"

Buck grunted and opened the door for Merry and Cait. "Fifteen minutes."

Chapter Five

Buck swung the truck around in front of the ranch house and saw Merry sitting on the top step of the stairs braiding Cait's hair. Cait sat on the second step.

Amazing. She didn't even sit that still for Karen. Cait actually had her face up to the sun, not hidden, and was listening as Merry spoke.

The psychiatrists couldn't understand why Cait hadn't spoken for so long. They suggested that everyone act normal, that someday she'd come around and not to push her. They tried to get to the reason why she wouldn't talk, but it just pushed her further into withdrawal.

So every day for two years, he'd tried to act normal, whatever that meant.

Mostly, he tried to make himself scarce, so as not to make Cait uncomfortable. He knew she blamed him for Debbie's leaving them, leaving her. Maybe someday she'd figure out the truth about Debbie: that she'd left her then four-year-old daughter to follow her own dream. Debbie had chosen fame over motherhood, a singing career instead of life on a cattle ranch.

He pulled a rubber band from around a stack of overdue bills he'd picked up at the post office and tossed them back on the dashboard. He used the rubber band to pull his own wet hair back into a ponytail.

In his haste to get to the hospital to see Karen, he had barely toweled off from his shower. Running a hand over the stubble on his face, he thought about going back to the bunkhouse to grab his shaver. He checked the clock. No time.

He got out of the truck and opened the door for Cait and Merry. Without him saying a thing, Cait got up from the step. He knew better than to help her into the truck, she'd only pull away from his touch.

Cait settled herself on the bench seat. He leaned in and smiled. "You look as beautiful as a rose this morning, honey."

Cait just stared ahead without acknowledging he spoke. He let out a deep breath. Maybe someday…

"I just have to get my purse," Merry yelled, disappearing into the house.

Soon she came running down the stairs, her golden hair catching glints from the sun. She smiled and looked as happy as she had earlier when she was talking about tropical French toast and maple biscuits with Cookie.

But the smile died on her lips as she froze in place. She looked down at the ground. Buck knew that she was about to scream, and he braced himself for when she exploded.

Snake?

He rushed to her, his eyes scanning the ground. He glanced at the potted plants, the stairs, the porch. No snake. Nothing.

"What is it?" he asked. She wasn't moving. "Merry?" She didn't answer. Carefully, he walked toward her and put a hand on her shoulder. "What's wrong?"

"My sh-shoe."

He looked down at her fuchsia-polished toes and her sandals consisting of thin straps of brown leather. "Yeah, you ought to wear something a little more substantial on your feet around here."

"My f-foot."

"What?" Her face had lost all color, and she was breathing hard. "What's wrong with your foot?"

"A l-lizard. It slithered over my foot and then ran off."

"How big?" Buck already knew the answer, but he wanted to get her talking and out of her shock.

"Huge." She stretched her arms as if showing him the fish that got away.

He laughed and the length of the lizard shrunk to about four inches as the seconds ticked by.

"Those are harmless," he said. "That little lizard is more afraid of you than you are of him. You'll see them around here all the time."

"Can't you get an exterminator?"

"They have every right to be here. Maybe even more than you do."

Damn. He could have kicked himself the second the words were out. The color was coming back into her face, all except around those lush lips, now pinched together.

"I meant—"

"I know exactly what you meant. This is the second time you told me that I don't belong here, Mr. Porter. However, as I told you before, I made a promise to a dear friend that I'd help her launch her business. Now that friend is ill and in the hospital, and I'd like to see her." She walked toward the truck without a glance back. "Shall we go?"

He had to give her credit. A little harmless lizard scared her to death, yet she could stand up to a tough cowboy like himself. He liked that. "Yes, Miss Turner. Let's go."

They didn't speak for a good twenty miles. Finally, Buck broke the silence. "I didn't mean what you think I meant."

"You meant every word."

Another five miles went by and Buck remembered that he neglected to give Merry a message. "Shoot. I forgot to tell you that your mother called. Well, her secretary called." He stole a glance at her at a red light, and her lips had formed into a thin line. "Hey, I'm really sorry. I picked up the phone in the barn, and didn't have anything to write with. But it wasn't an emergency. You're just supposed to call your mother at her office when you get a chance."

Now she looked deflated, as if something had sucked all the air out of her. He'd rather that she'd be mad at him than look like that.

"I'm not upset with you, Buck. Don't worry about it. It's just that…well, it's nothing."

She fussed with what looked like an expensive ruby-and-diamond ring that he'd bet cost more than a good bull.

"I'll return my mother's call later."

There was more silence, and he wondered what kind of mother would have her secretary call her own daughter. They must do things different in Boston than they do in Lizard Rock.

Lucking out on a big parking space near the hospital entrance, he centered his pickup.

"We'd better hurry," Merry said, echoing his thoughts.

They rushed through the hospital and walked into Karen's room. She looked as white as the sheet she was lying on. She gave a faint smile and a limp wave. He hated to see his energetic sister so ill.

"Hi." Karen's voice was barely a whisper. "You didn't have to come."

"We sure did," Buck said.

Merry went to the side of Karen's bed. "Of course we did."

"Hi, Caitlin. How about a hug?" Karen asked.

Caitlin didn't move.

"Cait, how are you getting along with Merry?" Karen pressed.

No answer.

"Doesn't her hair look beautiful?" Buck asked Karen. "Merry arranged it."

Cait touched a braid, and his heart skipped a beat. At last Cait had reacted to something he'd said.

Karen's eyes met his, and he struggled to keep his hand at his side, and not punch the air in happiness. It might be a small thing to her psychiatrist, but it wasn't to him.

Merry shook her finger at Cait, and grinned. "I do not want you laughing about the lizard that ran over my foot. Okay, Cait?"

Cait was wordless, but her eyes were brighter. Cait knew that Merry was joking with her.

Merry absentmindedly ran a hand over Cait's hair, and Buck noticed that Cait didn't pull away, or flinch from her touch like she did with everyone else.

"Cait's probably used to the little lizards, but I was petrified," Merry continued. "But Buck came to my rescue for the second time in just as many days."

"Good. I'm glad that my brother is taking care of you."

Merry met his gaze, raised an eyebrow and said, "He's been wonderful. He's made me feel right at home."

She was lying through her teeth so Karen wouldn't worry, and Buck could have kissed her right then and there. Their eyes met, and he nodded his thanks. Then he resolved to treat her better and keep his remarks to himself.

"Would you mind covering me with the blanket?" Karen asked.

Buck reached for the flannel blanket at the foot of

the bed at the same time as Merry did. Her hand closed over his, and then sprang away as if she'd actually touched the lizard that had run across her foot earlier.

She stared at him with a look of surprise on her face. He was just as shocked. Somehow that accidental touch just about knocked him out of his boots.

Was that something igniting between them, or was she recoiling as if she just walked into a tarantula convention? Whatever it was, it might be worth pursing. Either that, or he should hop on Bandit and head for the mountains.

Karen cleared her throat. "How about that blanket?"

"I'll get it," he said before Merry awoke from her trance.

What was it lately with women and him? His wife walked out, his daughter wouldn't look at him or talk, and now his simple touch had turned Merry into concrete.

A nurse came into the room and smiled at Buck. "Why, Buck Porter, it's been a long, long time."

"Hi, Cindy." He had graduated from Lizard Rock High School with Cindy Smith, now Cindy Devlin.

"You look scathingly handsome as usual."

That took some of the sting out of Merry's reaction. He remembered what a good barrel racer Cindy had been. She and his sister Louise always had a friendly competition going in high school as to who could win the most gold buckles.

"Thanks, Cindy."

Cindy turned to Merry. "Oh, excuse me. Is this *Mrs.* Bucklin Porter?"

Merry looked like she was ready to jump out the

window at the thought. "No," he said. "This is Meredith Bingham Turner, a friend of Karen."

"Of course. *Making Merry with Merry.*" She pulled out a pad and pen from the pocket of her uniform. "Could I have your autograph?"

"I'd be glad to. Is that Cindy with a *Y?*"

"Yes."

Buck watched as Merry wrote on the pad. He guessed she really was a celebrity.

"I just love your sausage balls, Merry. I made them for Christmas last year and they were a big hit."

"I like how they can be made early and then frozen." Merry handed back her pad. "Then all you have to do is pop them in the oven for fifteen minutes."

"And not be stuck in the kitchen all night."

"Exactly."

Buck rolled his eyes at Karen. She grinned back at him.

Cindy picked up the metal clipboard that was hanging from the foot of Karen's bed and leafed through it. "Well, back to business. I'm going to have to ask you all to leave. I have to prep Karen for surgery."

Finally. He'd been wondering if this was a hospital or a recipe exchange.

"Sis—" he grinned down at her "—I'll be thinking of you."

"Me, too," Merry added, holding out her hand to Caitlin to join them. Cait took her hand. "Buck, Cait and I won't leave until we find out how your surgery went."

"No. Go home," Karen said to Buck. "It's going to

be a long time. You have a ranch to run." She turned to Merry. "And the painters are supposed to be back today."

"Cookie'll let them in," Buck said. "You're more important to me than the ranch."

Karen looked up at Buck. "I didn't think anything was more important to you than the ranch."

He looked at Cait, who was still holding Merry's hand. "Well, you're wrong."

Cindy waved them toward the door. "Okay, shoo."

Buck gave his sister a thumbs-up sign before Cindy closed the door behind them.

They walked to the waiting room where four older men in cowboy hats were playing cards. Buck saw that one wall of the room had a row of pay phones. Another wall had vending machines.

Merry must have noticed the phones. "I might as well call my mother."

He nodded and sat next to Cait on an orange vinyl sofa. He reached for a crumpled newspaper on the end table, then handed Cait a book with a fairy on the front. Out of the corner of his eye, he watched Merry dial a series of numbers.

"Connie? It's Merry. I'm returning my mother's call. Yes, I'll hold." She studied her nails. "Hello, mother."

There was no emotion in her voice. It was as if she were ordering a pizza to go.

"No, mother. Yes, mother. I needed a vacation, Mother. I'm sorry you feel that way. Yes, I know I have responsibilities to my company, but Karen needs me for a few days." She took a deep breath.

She stood taller and tapped the metal of a shelf with a couple of fingers. To be nagged long distance on your own quarter was almost as bad as being kicked in the head by Bandit.

"For heaven's sake, mother, Karen doesn't live in a mud house. It's a very beautiful ranch house. Karen's mom was quite the talented artist. Her paintings are magnificent."

Buck held up the paper so she wouldn't notice that he was eavesdropping. He thought it was interesting that Merry referred to his mother as "mom" while addressing hers as "mother."

Merry closed her eyes and shook her head. "I'll call you again soon. No, I have not come into any contact with any reptiles or wild animals. Well, maybe just a small lizard. No, they do not frighten me. Not in the least."

He couldn't help himself. The laugh slipped out before he could choke it back.

She lowered her voice to a whisper, but he could still hear her. "I'll call you again soon. Give my best to Father. Goodbye."

The sound of her footsteps faded as she left the room.

Merry ordered two cups of coffee from the hospital cafeteria. "Give me the oldest and meanest cup of coffee you have. And I'll have a cup of hazelnut mocha. Both large, please." She decided to get something for Cait, too, and ordered a chocolate chip cookie, a bottle of apple juice and a bottle of water.

"Hey, aren't you Meredith Bingham Turner?" the girl behind the counter asked.

It always surprised her when she was recognized. "I am."

"I'm Janice. I watch your TV show all the time. I made your eucalyptus wreath for Christmas last year and your pinecone cornucopia centerpiece for Thanksgiving. I received a lot of compliments on them both."

"That's good to hear."

"You're not sick, are you?" Janice asked.

"I'm fine, thanks. I'm just visiting a friend."

Janice handed over the two cups of coffee in a cardboard tray. Merry reached into her purse for her wallet, but Janice waved her along.

"It's my treat. My boyfriend proposed to me after I served him your chicken pie with the mashed potato crust. We're going to be married in the spring, and I owe it all to you."

Merry laughed. "I doubt that, but congratulations, Janice."

This was why she used to love her work. She liked that she was helping others make their homes more comfortable and, well, homey.

With a sigh, she remembered that her business ventures were careening out of control. It was her fault. Riding the wave of her success, she had expanded too fast into too many things. Her main focus—hospitality and culinary arts—had fallen by the wayside.

With every step back to the waiting room, she tried to forget her mother's comments. Her mother had made it clear that Merry was wasting her time in Arizona—even neglecting her "empire."

In her younger years, she lived in eternal hope for

one genuine hug from them or, heaven forbid, one declaration of love for their only child.

No matter what she did, it was never good enough for either her mother or father. All through her life, she'd had only criticism from them, never compliments. But she'd created her own business in spite of them, and she was damn proud of what she'd accomplished.

Well, her so-called empire could just wait. Karen needed her here. And Karen was her best friend, but her mother would never understand that.

Karen had dragged her to her first hockey game, where Merry had screamed for the Boston Bruins so loud that she lost her voice. She'd also taken Merry to her first frat party, where she danced the night away and almost lost her virginity—but Karen got her away from the drunken preppie. They took long walks on Charlestown Beach where they rented a little cottage by the ocean during spring breaks. They shared their dreams, their hopes.

And little by little, Karen had pulled Merry out of her introverted shell.

They even discussed going to go into business together; Merry, the culinary and hospitality arts major, and Karen, the business and floral design major. They talked about a combination hotel or bakery/café/floral shop, or even a luxury hotel and spa near the ocean, maybe on Block Island or Point Judith. Or maybe even in Boston. But all their dreams and plans fell through when Karen had decided to go back to Arizona and help out at the ranch.

Karen had always talked about her family, and

Merry was green with envy as to how close they were. Karen had showed her pictures when she came back from semester breaks or Christmas vacations. And, yes, Merry had always thought that Karen's older brother was a hunk. But Buck had gotten taller and stronger and even more handsome through the years, and those pictures didn't come close to capturing the sheer masculinity that radiated from him in person.

She returned to the waiting room to find Buck pacing, his long legs making travel quick. She set the apple juice in front of Cait, but it was the cookie that Meredith handed her that made her eyes twinkle slightly.

Turning to Buck, she gave him one of the coffee cups. "I thought you could use some gun cleaner."

Grateful, he reached for the cup she handed him. "You're a wonderful woman."

"Remember those words when I'm planning the dude ranch and screaming about burros and lizards and snakes."

"But I just heard you say you have no reptile or animal problems whatsoever," he teased.

Meredith was quiet for a moment. "The Turners wouldn't win any prizes for family of the year."

"Sorry, I couldn't help but hear," Buck said. "If I were a gentleman, I would have left the room, but no one's ever accused me of being a gentleman. Besides, Cait was reading a book."

She waved away his apology. "Don't worry about it."

He sat down and so did she. He pulled the lid back from his coffee and took a tentative draw. "Great stuff."

He hesitated for a moment, put the cup on the table and leaned toward her with his hands clasped. "Do you want to talk about it?"

"The coffee?"

"The call."

No, she didn't want to. "You wouldn't understand."

"Try me. We have a couple of hours to kill."

She took a deep breath and let it out slowly. "You were raised in a close, loving family and I wasn't. That's all there is to say. I was a lonely…I mean *only*…an *only* child."

"Freudian slip?"

"You know Freud?"

"I know cattle and ranching. I don't profess to know much more than that, but I do know that was one heavy-duty conversation you had with your mother."

Her heart was fluttering and she knew her cheeks were on fire.

Why did this man get to her so?

One minute she was ready to strangle him, the next second she wanted to tell him her deepest thoughts and feel his strong arms around her, comforting her. Other times his touch made her so nervous, she could jump out of her skin.

It was almost as if he could see clear through to her soul already, and she didn't like it. More than once she had confided in a man, and he turned around and told the tabloids for the whole world to know.

She'd vowed never to let her guard down like that again. She had an image to maintain as a strong and capable woman.

But Buck's eyes seemed to see right through her. And he could be so sweet. He'd slept on the couch for his daughter. He loved his family. He loved his ranch. He loved his troubled daughter.

But why would he expect that she'd talk about her innermost problems with a six-year-old present?

She looked at Cait, who was sitting motionless, staring at the cover of the book. There were cookie crumbs all over her face. Merry opened the bottle of water, took out a tissue and wet it.

She handed Cait the tissue. "Here you go, cookie face."

Without a word, Cait began to wipe her mouth.

"You're beautiful again, Cait Porter." Merry held out her hand, and Cait set the tissue carefully in her palm. When Merry handed Cait the bottle of apple juice, the little girl took a long drink.

Merry got up and sat between Buck and Cait. "Sweetie, would you like me to read that book to you? It looks interesting."

She noticed that Cait loosened her grip on the sides of the book, and Merry slowly took it. She read the cover, *"The Fairy Princess of the Flowers,"* then opened to page one. "You know, Cait, your aunt Karen loves flowers. You have beautiful flowers all around your house."

She turned to see Buck smiling at her, and it just about curled her toes.

He moved his arm and rested it on the top of the couch, his hand hung down, and she could feel his fingers lightly brushing her shoulder. The charge from his touch was so intense, Merry could barely concentrate on the fairy princess.

She forced herself to move slowly away from his touch. They were in a public place, and some people in the hospital had already recognized her. If there were cameras or reporters around, she didn't want her picture taken with him touching her, which would surely incite a tabloid frenzy. There was no need for Buck and Cait to be subjected to that kind of chaos.

But if Merry was honest with herself, this was only half the truth. The other half was the fact that she was attracted to Buck, and there was no future in it for either of them.

Chapter Six

Buck was stiff and sore from sitting, but he didn't want to step away from the waiting room and miss the doctor. Merry was curled up on the couch across from him. Cait was curled up on the opposite side of his couch, but wasn't really sleeping. He had snagged a hospital blanket and pillow for both of them.

Right now, the proper Bostonian was snoring, and his daughter was glancing at him from time to time.

"Would you like me to read another book to you, Cait? I see one about a pony over there. He looks like your pony, doesn't he?"

Cait just closed her eyes.

Buck's heart sank. What would it take to get through to her? When would his daughter come back to him? Hadn't he been punished enough?

He was in the middle of peeling the wrapper off of a candy bar that Cait had refused when Dr. Goodwater walked in. Buck stood.

"It went without a hitch. Karen will be fine."

As relief replaced worry, Buck grabbed the doctor's hand and shook it. "Thanks."

"We're going to keep an eye on her for a few days. Then she'll need to do a lot of resting at home, but we'll talk about that later."

"Can I see her?"

"She's still in Recovery. I'll tell Cindy to let you know when she's back in her room."

"Thanks again, Doc."

"Just wait till you get my bill."

He motioned for Buck to follow him to the hall.

"How's Caitlin doing?" the doctor whispered.

"The same. She still doesn't talk, doesn't laugh. She still hides." Buck looked away. "I don't know what to do anymore. I've gone broke taking her to psychiatrists, but if you have another idea, I'll find more money."

The doctor gripped Buck's shoulder. "I don't, Buck. I'll keep asking around, but maybe all she needs is more time."

"It's been two years since Debbie left. How much longer?"

"I just don't know. It's out of my field of expertise."

"I know. But thanks for asking."

Dr. Goodwater shook his head and hurried off.

Buck needed to call Louise at school and get a message to Ty up at the line shack and tell them that

Karen was going to be fine. He walked back into the waiting room to use the pay phone.

Merry stirred and opened an eye. "Karen?"

"She's fine. The doctor was just here. We can see her soon."

"Wonderful. I'm so glad." Sitting up, she pushed her hair back and squinted against the glare of the fluorescent lights.

As disheveled as she was, she still looked beautiful. He had an urge to run his hands over her hair and smooth it back into place, but he headed for the phone instead.

Louise answered right away.

"Karen's fine, Lou. She's going to be in the hospital for a few days yet. You'd better stay put and take your bar exam or she'll have your head. I'll get a message to Ty. You take care and come home when you can. Later, Lou."

"What's it like having brothers and sisters?" Merry asked when he sat back down.

"Mostly good."

"As I understand it, the three of them want the dude ranch and you don't. Right?"

"Right as rain."

She raised a perfect eyebrow. "Then what *do* you want?"

He thought for a while. It was hard to put everything into words, especially to someone who'd never understand. He wanted Cait to be the girl she used to be. And he'd love more kids. He'd teach them how to ride and to appreciate the land, but he wouldn't make them feel guilty if they chose another path of life. He wanted the ranch to stay the way it was, but that wasn't going to happen. He wanted a wife who adored him and loved the ranch, too. He wanted his debt gone and needed the capital to expand into rodeo-stock contracting. He wanted to hire more help.

"I have a whole list." He looked at Caitlin, now sitting up and looking at the pony book that she didn't want him to read to her. His daughter was at the top of that list.

Sure, there was a whole litany of things he wanted, but none of them were going to happen unless his gallery sale was a huge success or he decided to sell that big plot of land on the Rattlesnake River to a developer.

But if he did that, the remaining part of his ranch wouldn't support the stock he wanted to bring in. It was a no-win situation.

Merry would never understand all this. She'd had a rich upbringing and now led a glamorous life. She could buy whatever she wanted, whenever she wanted.

He saw Cindy motioning to him. It was time to see his sister.

Karen was groggy. She mustered a smile and not much more. "Go home. Let me sleep. Come back tomorrow night."

"I'll stay with you." Merry looked up at Buck, wondering what he wanted to do.

"Go," Karen said, shooting her brother a frustrated look. "All of you."

"She means business when she has that look." He put his hand over Karen's, and she closed her eyes. "We'd better hit the road."

Looking at the monitors and IV drips, Merry remembered when she'd had her appendix out. She'd been seven, and her parents had her in a private room with no one to talk to. They had visited her briefly after work, but during the day she was so very scared and all alone. One of the nurses had felt sorry for her and would keep her company, but her parents hadn't missed an hour of work from their brokerage. It was something that she'd never forget as long as she lived.

They'd sent her a bouquet of daisies with balloons, but her mother had never pushed her hair back from her face or never wiped her tears. They'd given her a pretty blue satin nightgown and bathrobe that made her feel like a princess, but she would have traded it gladly for a hug and a kiss from them.

"You ladies say your goodbyes. I'll wait outside with Cait."

Merry held her hand out to Cait. "Don't you want to say goodbye to Aunt Karen?"

Cait slowly walked over to her aunt's beside, but looked down at the ground.

"Bye, honey," Karen said. "You be good for your daddy and Merry."

Cait turned and walked to the door. Merry doubted if the girl had it in her to be bad.

Merry kissed Karen's cheek and whispered, "Don't worry about a thing. The painters will finish up soon, and my camera crew and photographer are arriving tomorrow. I plan on using Buck for the commercial and a brochure." She added with a twang, "With a little beefcake from Bucklin Floyd Porter, the city gals will be stampeding out to the Rattlesnake Dude Ranch in the hope of lassoing a cowboy hunk."

Karen's eyes flew open. "Did Buck agree to that?"

"Not exactly," Merry admitted, "but I plan on asking him soon."

Karen gave a weak half smile. "I wish I could be a fly on the wall when you do."

Figuring that meant she had Karen's approval, she continued. "I just plan on interviewing Buck for the commercial clip. I figure we can walk around the ranch as we shoot it and show some of the beautiful scenery and, of course, the house. We can use my interview with him as a voice-over. Publicity should be our number-one concern right now."

"Whatever you do is fine with me. I just wish I could be there to watch." Karen's eyes darted to her brother, who was standing by the door talking to Cindy. "Um…about Buck," she whispered. "When God passed out pride and stubbornness, Buck got in line twice."

"I already figured that out. Don't worry about a thing. I'll treat him gently. You just get some rest."

"And Cait…" Karen's eyes fluttered shut.

Merry reached for her friend's hand and gave it a squeeze. "Don't worry. I'll take care of both of them."

"I'll make you an early dinner. You really haven't had anything to eat all day," Merry said as she got out of the truck.

"You don't have to bother," Buck replied. "I'll grab a sandwich at the bunkhouse later." He started toward the barn. "Right now I have to take care of the horses."

"Please, let me make you both dinner," she said. "I have something I need to ask you."

He hesitated, then nodded. "Okay. Give me an hour or so," he said, checking his watch. "C'mon, Cait."

Cait didn't move. Instead she walked up the steps to the ranch and waited at the front door for Merry.

"Damn," Buck mumbled.

"Don't worry. I'll watch her. Maybe she'll help me cook."

"That'll be the day." He pushed back his hat with a thumb. "But I'd appreciate you keeping an eye on her."

"I'll enjoy it." Merry hurried up the stairs, found the key under the flowerpot and opened the door.

"Do you want to help me cook, Cait?" she asked. "I need someone who can show me where things are. I'd appreciate your help, if you don't mind."

Cait proceeded into the kitchen, and Merry took it as a good sign. She wasn't going to force the girl into anything, but maybe they could work together.

Merry could create something fabulous in an hour.

Merry stared into the refrigerator, calculating what she could make out of the contents. "Let's see, Cait. We have lots of veggies in here. That's probably your aunt Karen's doing. She likes her veggies. I see some boneless chicken, too. How about if we make a stir-fry?" She turned back to Cait, who was sitting at the table, staring straight ahead. "Would you and your daddy eat stir-fry? You know, veggies and chicken, maybe over rice?"

Cait got up, walked over to the refrigerator, leaned over and pointed to a pack of flour tortillas and some hamburger. Then she retreated back to her chair.

Merry tried not to overreact, but it was the first time that Cait had really tried to communicate. "Okay. Burritos. I got it. You are right, Cait. Your dad isn't the stir-fry type. Beef and bean burritos. Perfect."

Merry kicked off her sandals, began frying the meat and peeling and chopping onions.

"How about setting the table, Cait? Can you do that? I just don't know where anything is."

Cait got up, opened a drawer and took out rust-colored place mats. She positioned three on the table.

Merry hummed as she fluttered around. She loved to cook and fuss, but this was even better. This time she was cooking for Buck and Cait.

She froze and tried to analyze the difference. Maybe it was because Cait and Buck seemed to need a little TLC at the moment. Maybe it was because cooking for real people was so much better than cooking for a TV camera, or because Karen had asked her to take care of them.

Merry suspected that it was because she could pretend that they were her family and this was her house for a while.

She couldn't pinpoint the exact source of her happiness, but she planned on enjoying it while it lasted.

Merry clicked the radio on, and sang along with a popular country song. Cait looked at her, her eyes as wide as the plates that she'd just set the table with. Merry thought the girl was either ready to bolt or ready to scream.

"Is my singing that bad?" Merry grinned and put her hands on her hips.

Cait ignored her and proceeded to set out the silverware. Merry went over to the table and sat down. "How about if I showed you how to fold the napkins into fancy shapes?"

Cait gave a slight nod.

"I'll show you how to make a pointy hat. First you fold the napkin in half, like this. Then you bring the two sides together and tuck them in, like this."

Cait's eyes studied her every move as she folded the napkin. "I once did a dinner party for twenty people, and made swans out of the napkins. If you want, I can show you that sometime." She was talking and Cait was listening, and she felt like she was making progress with the girl. "Now you try it. I have to check the stove."

Merry went back to singing. Out of the corner of her eye, she saw Cait make another hat. It was perfect. She set it in the middle of the place mat in front of her.

"Excellent hat, Cait," Merry said, chopping another onion. "Maybe you could make an extra hat for Aunt Karen. You could bring it to her tomorrow at the hospital." She started another song.

Even over her singing, she could hear the mudroom door open and the thump of boots hitting the floor.

Cait stopped working on the napkins and put her hands in her lap. Judging by her unfavorable reaction, it must be Buck.

She finished her song and the onion and noticed him standing in the mudroom and leaning against the doorframe leading into the kitchen. He was in his stocking feet and his big toes were sticking out of holes in his socks.

He, too, looked wide-eyed at her singing, and Merry decided that her voice must be worse than she thought.

"Don't stop on my account," he said, his blue eyes twinkling.

"If you value your eardrums, be glad I did."

He sniffed the air. "It smells good. I guess I'm mighty hungry after all."

"It's ready. Please, have a seat."

His chair scraped on the floor as he sat down at the kitchen table. He held up a napkin hat. "Did you make these, Cait?"

The girl was silent.

He whistled. "That's mighty clever. Looks like my cowboy hat, don't you think?"

More silence.

Looking for a bowl in the cupboards, Merry found one she wanted just out of reach. Pulling over a chair, she stood on it.

"Don't fall," Buck warned.

She felt his hands on her waist and she jumped at his unexpected touch. She handed him the bowl she wanted, and he set it down on the counter.

He lifted her down from the chair as if she weighed nothing at all. She backed away from him, stunned at the heat that flooded her body. She felt flushed and suddenly boneless, but she wanted Buck's hands back where they were, and then some. The cheery kitchen became heavy with tension, each of them trying to decide what to do next.

He returned to normal first, and sat back down at the table. After some light conversation—and his third helping of burritos—she decided the time was right to ask him.

She didn't like excluding Cait from the conversation, though. "I was going to make stir-fry, but Cait said you'd like the burritos better."

Buck leaned forward. *"What?"*

Merry nodded. "Well, she showed me—in the refrigerator. So that's what I made instead."

He seemed totally taken aback by the news, and his eyes brightened as he looked at Cait. "Thank you, Cait. I like burritos a lot."

Cait didn't lift her head and kept on eating. Nevertheless, Buck seemed happy, so Merry decided that she might as well take advantage of his cheerful mood and jump right in.

"Buck, I'd like to ask for a favor. My photographer and a camera crew are coming tomorrow. I'd like you to be the model for the brochure of the dude ranch and be in the commercial. Cait can be in the pictures, too, if she'd like."

Cait got up from the table and put her plate and fork in the dishwasher. Returning to the table, she took her little stack of napkin hats and left the kitchen. Merry heard the TV go on in the living room.

She watched as Buck put his fork down, leaned back in the chair and crossed his arms in front of his chest. His body language told her that she didn't have a prayer of getting his cooperation.

She dove right in. "For the commercial, I figure the best approach will be just a brief walk through the ranch, with the two of us walking together, chatting around the property. We can cut it down to the best footage."

"Chatting?" He picked up his plate, walked over to the sink, rinsed it off and put it in the dishwasher. "I don't chat."

"You'd be perfect," Merry said, turning in her chair to face him. "I thought that the second I saw you."

He raised an eyebrow, obviously amused. "Oh, yeah?"

"Your blue eyes are killer. And a couple of shots of you with your shirt off shoveling hay, well…" She suddenly realized that she'd said too much.

He smiled knowingly. His eyes pinned her with a gaze so intense, she couldn't breathe. "So, you've been watching me, Miss Turner?"

His voice was throaty. Sexy. A shiver went through her.

"Well, not exactly." She tried to look anywhere but at him. "I was looking at you from a purely business standpoint."

"But you liked what you saw? From a purely business standpoint, that is."

"Yes. I mean no."

He raised an eyebrow.

"I mean yes." How did she get into this mess? "I just think you'd make a perfect model for the brochure and you'd be perfect for the commercial. That's all there is to it. And it'll save money if you'll do it instead of me having to hire someone."

"You mean you were thinking of paying for a model?"

"Of course."

"Damn. I'm not paying for a damn model."

"You don't have to. I will."

His eyes narrowed. "The Porters don't take charity."

"It's not charity. Karen can pay me back out of the profits. With my connections, I figure I can get a model for about five hundred dollars an hour, plus expenses." She knew that would get him.

He raked his fingers through his hair. "For cryin' out loud. This whole thing is getting out of hand." He seemed ready to make a quick exit.

"All you have to do is go about your regular business and my photographer and cameraman will be as unobtrusive as possible and take some shots of you. And then we'll chat together for the commercial."

Buck would undoubtedly be miserable through the whole thing, but she was prepared for that. He was silent, but shifted on his feet as if he was deciding what to do.

"Dammit. All right. I'll do it if it'll save the money."

She knew she'd backed him into a corner, but no one could represent the spirit of the Rattlesnake Ranch better than Buck.

"It won't be all that bad," she said, hoping to placate him.

"Yes, it will," he snapped, heading for the door. Then he stopped and turned toward her. "Merry, would you mind seeing that Cait gets to bed by eight-thirty? I have to drive up to the line shack and update Ty about Karen. I should be back before then, but in case I'm not…"

"I'd be glad to watch Cait. Go ahead."

"Thanks for dinner. I'll be back as soon as I can."

He clamped his hat on his head, grabbed his boots and was gone before she could say another word.

Chapter Seven

Buck slipped behind the wheel of his pickup. He could have easily sent one of the hands or another one of the hands with the message for Ty, but he wanted to do it himself. He needed to do some thinking and let off a little steam.

A model? Him? He was a *rancher* for heaven's sake. He punched the top of the dashboard with his closed fist.

The pain that shot up his arm didn't make him feel better, but the other things that Merry had said made him grin. There wasn't a doubt in his mind that she had been looking at him—and liking what she saw.

Killer blue eyes?

And she had been thinking about him without his shirt on.

He thought of Merry in the tree bed yet again. How he'd like to join her there and wondered what it'd be like if they made love.

Was there a passionate woman under her uptight, businesslike demeanor?

He heard a rumble of thunder and saw lightning flash in the distance. A storm must be brewing. Just like the storm that was churning in his mind.

He hadn't stopped thinking of Merry since he'd met her. She'd behaved foolishly with those burros and the lizard, but it made him want to protect her. He liked the way she'd brought him coffee in the morning, even if it was flavored. How she was able to get some reaction from his daughter.

If Merry could only get Cait to open up a little more, he'd be eternally grateful.

But she was a TV star. He was only a rancher. There was no future for them. He had nothing to offer her, no more than he'd had to offer Lisa Daniels, who turned down his offer of marriage, or Debbie Dalton, who'd accepted—and then divorced him.

He remembered the night he was going to ask Lisa to marry him. It was on a Friday night at Gordo's, a bar in Mountain Springs. He was just about to pop the big question when Lisa informed him that she was breaking up with him.

The Wednesday before, she'd met a wealthy plastic surgeon while she was waiting tables at the Road Runner Restaurant and was leaving to join him in California on Monday.

Then there was Debbie, his ex-wife. She wasn't as

kind. One afternoon, she told him that she'd met a Nash-ville record producer while Buck was in Phoenix with Caitlin. The producer convinced Debbie that he'd make her the next Reba McEntire.

There was an ugly scene in the barn, with Debbie yelling and him yelling back.

Debbie's words still echoed in his mind. "I never wanted this life, Buck, but you went and got me pregnant. Now I'm stuck with a brat and a husband that's never going to amount to anything."

Debbie had never looked back. She got what she wanted, he supposed. Her records were climbing the charts, she'd made a couple of videos and had per-formed on a country-music awards show.

And he'd got his divorce papers in the mail almost immediately after her departure.

Since Lisa and Debbie, he'd made it a habit not to get involved in a serious relationship. Maybe a nice little mutual pleasure with Meredith Bingham Turner was just what he needed.

A fling with Merry could only be that—a fling—and nothing more. They were just too different. Plus, he already knew that when it came to money, control and ambition, Merry made Lisa and Debbie look like amateurs.

Clouds of dust swirled in front of him. He lowered his speed and flipped on the radio to hear the weather report and to distract himself from more thoughts of Merry.

"Heavy rains moving in," the announcer said. "No unnecessary travel and stay out of the washes." Buck could see lightning off to the right, over the Dead Horse Mountains.

He shouldn't have left Cait and Merry alone. Merry had probably never experienced a monsoon before, with its torrential rain and the accompanying light-and-sound show. No doubt she'd be scared out of her wits. Caitlin would be scared, too.

Normally, he'd radio Cookie or the boys in the bunk-house to check on them, but they'd all gone to town tonight to raise a little hell and hear the Lizard Rock Cowboys play.

Buck would probably be back before the worst of it started. As long as he could reach the top of Indian Bonnet Butte, he'd be able to reach Ty on the CB and tell him about Karen. Cell phones just didn't work out here.

Buck liked the monsoon season. He loved to watch the forces of nature at work, as long as everyone was safe and secure and not on the roads or out in it.

And Merry sure was something to watch, too.

Damn, there she was, intruding on his thoughts again.

The wind picked up and the rain started pummeling the truck as if thousands of horseshoes were being thrown at it. He pulled over to the side of the road, deciding to turn back. Just as he did, he heard a horn beeping, and Ty's dark green pickup pulled up alongside his.

Buck rolled down his window. The rain poured into the truck and onto his face and arm.

"What the hell are you doing out in this, big brother?"

"I was hoping to get close enough to reach you on the CB and tell you about Karen."

"What's wrong?" Ty yelled over the noise.

"Her operation was moved up. Emergency situation. It's over, and she's fine now."

"Great." Ty wiped the water from his face with his shirtsleeve. "Meet you back at the house. You can tell me more."

"Wait." Buck wanted to tell him that they had a guest and not to go charging into the house half cocked or he'd scare Merry, but Ty was already on his way, driving way too fast as usual.

He swore and wondered if he would have been as carefree and as reckless as Ty if he hadn't been stuck with so much responsibility at such a young age.

Well, maybe *stuck* wasn't exactly the right word. He just did what he had to do.

If he had the money, he'd ask Ty or one of his sisters if they'd take over the reins of the ranch for a while. He wanted to sit on a beach somewhere and wile away the hours reading Zane Grey. Not too long, maybe a month or so would do it before he got bored out of his mind, but it sure would be nice.

He hadn't been off the ranch for eight or nine years, with the exception of a couple of rodeos or bull-riding events when he needed some quick money. As much as he loved the Rattlesnake, he had to admit that he could use a break—from everything.

But Karen had dropped plenty of hints about starting her own florist shop and nursery in town some day. Lou had plans to hang out her own shingle. Ty still wasn't sure what he was going to do, but he had a restlessness inside him that would keep him wandering. Which left the full responsibility of running the ranch on Buck's weary shoulders.

Not to mention the added task of keeping an eye on Meredith Bingham Turner and making sure she didn't dress up his ranch—his home—in ribbons and bows.

As he cut the motor in front of the house, he heard a familiar scream. Then he saw Ty running down the porch stairs just as a pot headed for the back of his skull. He slid on the last step and fell face forward into a puddle as the pan clanked down the stairs and landed with a splash next to him.

Ty looked up and blinked, mud and rain dripping from his face. "Who was that?"

Buck laughed and offered a hand to help him up. "That, baby brother, is Meredith Bingham Turner, TV star and all-around celebrity, and the best screamer in all of the United States."

Buck sprang to his feet as the roar of a motor cut the early morning silence. Headlights shone through the picture window, lighting up the living room and blinding him. In a quest to find his jeans and a weapon, he fell over the coffee table and blurted his favorite expletive.

"What's all the noise?" Meredith appeared from the bedroom, robe in hand. Her eyes blinked in the glare of the lights until she shaded them with her hand like a sun visor. "What's going on?"

Buck froze in place, unable to take his eyes off her. She wore a slip of a nightgown in a blue-green color, which became transparent when she stood by the window. Her curves were outlined, and she looked unworldly, ethereal. He ached to run his hands over her skin, to touch every part of her... But first he needed to find out what the racket was all about.

Merry turned her attention to the window, and her nightgown became even more transparent. Finally, she slipped on her robe, which helped a little.

"I'm sorry they woke you up, Buck. It's my staff."

He looked at her. "Your what?"

She pointed. "There's Tim, my photographer, and that's Buzz, who's going to shoot the TV clip and the commercial." Her voice dropped to a whisper. "And Joanne, my new assistant and publicist."

Buck couldn't believe the intrusion. "What the hell are they all doing here at four o'clock in the damn morning?"

"I forgot to tell you." She slapped her forehead. "They flew in on a red-eye from Logan Airport and then drove from the Tucson airport. I'm surprised that they found the ranch in the dark."

"What luck," he snapped.

Buck knew he was crankier than the occasion deserved, but it had taken him hours to drift off to sleep on the couch after thinking about Merry all night, only to find himself dreaming of her. Now, after being rudely awakened—and seeing Merry looking all sleepy and sexy and silhouetted in the light so her nightclothes just about disappeared—he was more frustrated than ever.

It was starting off to be one hell of a day, and he knew it would only get worse when he had to pose for pictures.

"Cait's still sleeping." Merry grabbed a serape from the couch and wrapped it around herself. "I'll let them in and tell them to keep it down. Then I'll make us all some breakfast."

"Do what you've got to do. I'm headed for the bunkhouse."

"Please stay and meet them."

He didn't answer. He didn't want to meet anyone at this time of the morning no matter who they were.

He was never going to like strangers invading his house—not now, not ever.

He opened the front door to make his escape.

"Don't forget, you agreed to model," Merry whispered. "We're going to need you right after sunrise."

He bit back the reply that sprang to his lips.

As he hurried down the front stairs, it was all he could do to keep himself from jumping into his pickup, pointing it away from the Rattlesnake and stepping on the gas.

Merry could see the stunned expression on Joanne's face the second she saw Buck running down the stairs shirtless, shoeless and zipping up his jeans. He did manage to plop his hat on his head. The next second, Joanne's eyes became wider when she saw Merry adjusting her serape.

"That's some nightgown under that blanket," Joanne said.

Okay, it might be too much for the Rattlesnake Ranch, but she'd got the nightgown and robe on sale at Filene's and had tossed it in her suitcase without thinking.

Joanne took her by the arm and led her into the ranch house away from the gaping mouths of her staff.

"A cowboy?" Joanne asked, eyebrows raised.

Merry felt her face heat. "It's not what you think."

Joanne held up a finger in warning. "Let me remind you that I'm still running interference from your last indiscretion."

"Indiscretion?" She shook her head. "My personal life is my own business."

"Not when you're in the public eye. If you haven't noticed, the tabloids haven't gotten that message. They've had a field day with George Lynch and his kiss-and-tell tales."

Merry's stomach churned with anger. She wanted to scream at the woman. "Buck is my friend's brother. That's all. He's also going to be our model, and he's one of the owners of this ranch."

Joanne looked around the room and turned up her nose. "Just when I thought it couldn't get any worse."

Merry took a deep breath and counted to ten. They didn't think along the same lines, didn't mesh. But to her credit, Joanne had helped deflect some of the negative publicity surrounding George Lynch.

"Let me grab a quick shower and get changed," Merry finally said. "Please have the crew take some film and pictures of the sunrise and some other filler shots. I'd like everything done by this afternoon, so you can all head home."

"The sooner we're done, the better."

"Exactly," Merry said under her breath.

"What's going on at the homestead, big brother?" Buck poked his head out of the shower stall at the bunkhouse, and saw Ty pulling over a battered metal chair and stretching out his long, lanky legs. His sandy-brown hair needed a cut, and he was sporting two days' worth of beard. His eyes always twinkled, and trouble always found him, but when Ty wasn't brawling or chugging down a longneck, he was really a closet intellectual.

"Dammit, Ty, can't you give a man some privacy?"

His brother's grin was infectious, and Buck could never stay mad at Ty very long.

"So," Ty repeated, "what's going on?"

"Meredith Bingham Turner is off and running to change a ranch house into a dude ranch like you and the girls wanted. Her staff just rolled in."

"And that bothers you?"

He soaped his chest with a fury. "You know it does."

"You still have that failure thing going?"

"Failure thing?"

"The silly notion that you failed in your quest to keep the ranch the way it always was."

Buck stopped in mid-soap. He could deny it, but Ty hit the nail right on the head. "What? Are you going to be a shrink now?"

Ty shrugged his shoulders. "Two years ago I was going to be a botanist. Shrink was three years ago. This year, I'm taking the time off to figure out what I want to do."

"How time flies when I'm paying the bills."

"Big brother, I've taken out some loans myself and you know it. But talking about money is a bore, and I've been working off my debt here. But tell me about Meredith. She's quite the looker. Married? Single?"

"Single."

"Did you stake your claim already?"

"That's none of your business."

Ty rubbed his chin. "Hmm...I think you are definitely interested in her, Bucklin Floyd."

"Get the hell out of here and let me finish my shower. I need to look pretty this morning. I'm the damn model for the advertising brochure and whatever the hell else."

Buck knew he shouldn't have divulged that little tidbit of information. He'd never hear the end of it.

Ty got up slowly, but he struck quick. He grabbed Buck's cheek and pinched. "You're already pretty, Bucklin," he said, then fled as his brother lunged for him.

He's absolutely gorgeous, Merry thought as Buck approached the corral. His shoulders had never looked wider and his eyes had never looked bluer. A long-sleeved chambray shirt was tucked into jeans that he'd been born to wear, and Merry wondered if the shirt was as soft to the touch as it looked. His lean waist was circled by a brown leather belt with turquoise stones and conchos and was held together by a large, oval silver belt buckle that glistened in the sun.

He had a slight smile on his face, as if he had just heard a good joke. Maybe he wasn't as mad as she thought he'd be.

"We couldn't have hired anyone that perfect," Joanne whispered, just as Merry was thinking the same thing.

"Let's get this over with," Buck said to Merry. "What do you want me to do?"

Before she had a chance to answer, Joanne grabbed his arm and steered him toward the gate. "Let's pose you feeding the horses in the barn or something."

He glanced over his shoulder at Merry and she knew she had to rescue him.

"Joanne, I'll take care of this project. I promised Buck that we wouldn't pose him." She pointed to a picnic table. "How about if you set up the outdoor picnic scene? You'll find the things I want to use on the kitchen counter inside."

With Joanne again out of the way, Merry returned to Buck. He was leaning against the fence of the corral, looking at his horses. Now, this was a natural shot of a man who clearly enjoyed what he did. A man comfortable in his skin. Where on earth was her cameraman?

She took a deep breath. "I know I said that we wouldn't pose you, but how about a little shirtless hay forking, or whatever you call it? The sun's perfect overhead. I don't know how to ask this, so I'll come right to the point. Do you mind if I spray you with water? You know, so it looks like you're sweating?"

She couldn't quite meet his eyes.

He tweaked his hat with his thumb and index finger. "Cowboy beefcake shots?"

If she lived to be a hundred, she'd never forget the way Buck took his shirt off. The knowing smile, the tease in his eyes, his big, rough, sun-darkened hands dislodging the white buttons that seemed too tiny for such big fingers.

He pulled the shirt out of his jeans and her breath

caught. With several more flicks of buttons, it hung loosely at his sides.

"Gee, it's hot out here," she blurted, before she could stop herself.

"It's the desert."

She smiled at his old standby saying, trying to look casual. She tried to make herself look away, but this was something she wanted to remember long into those cold, lonely Boston nights.

"There's a hose in the garden," he said.

"For what?"

"I thought you wanted to spray me with water." His eyes sparked in amusement. He seemed to be enjoying this, or at least her discomfort.

Trying to control her breathing, she waited for what he was going to do next.

In one smooth movement, the shirt was off and he tossed it toward the fence. It hung over the rail neatly like a blue flag.

"Maybe the hose isn't really necessary," she said weakly.

"Whatever you say, but if you'll give me a couple of minutes and let me muck the stalls like I need to do, I can work up the genuine article in no time…real cowboy sweat."

Merry could feel her blood running hot through her veins. Buck was teasing her, and he knew exactly how he was affecting her.

She'd better get her mind back on business. She'd worked on shoots with male models a million times before, and she never usually blinked an eye.

But none of them were Buck.

He cleared his throat. He was standing with his hands on hips. She looked at his wide chest, his washboard stomach and muscular biceps. She wanted to run her hands over the smooth muscles of his chest and arms, wanted to know if his skin was as warm as she knew it'd be under the desert sun.

Whew!

She glanced down at the clipboard in front of her. It just had a smattering of notes, but her eyes couldn't focus.

It sure was hot in the desert.

Buck watched as Merry fussed with setting the old picnic table under the cottonwood tree. Even he could tell that the little touches she added to the picture portrayed the essence of the ranch.

She used a serape as a tablecloth, his mother's dishes, and the way she positioned the Pima blankets and pottery was something his mother might have done.

Tim kept his camera clicking from all angles. First, he had to stare at the mountains, holding a pitchfork over some hay. Then he had to stand with a saddle slung over his shoulder.

Merry had made a pot of chili and some corn bread for the table display and he had to admit that it smelled good enough to eat. She directed Tim to make sure that he captured the steam that came from the pot in his pictures. Then she said it was time for Buzz to film as they walked the grounds and talked.

She was damn easy to talk to. They leaned against the corral and he talked about the ranch. Then against the porch railing and told her how he wanted to buy some rodeo stock. On another occasion, they sat in front of the beehive fireplace, and he told her the story about the day that he and his dad designed it and then made it. Then they walked around the barn.

Finally, they were done. Merry suggested that they invite the ranch hands over to eat the "props."

So Cookie and the rest of the boys came running. Buck wasn't getting any work out of them, anyway, since they were too busy watching. They might as well eat and be in Tim's pictures and Buzz's movie.

"What's different about this chili?" Buck finally asked Merry after his third bowl. "I can't put my finger on it."

"It's turkey chili. I found a turkey breast in the freezer and—"

"Turkey?" Buck almost choked. "I'm a cattle rancher! Cattle. That means beef. Chili is made with beef."

The ranch hands laughed, with Ty laughing the loudest, but they didn't stop eating.

"But turkey is lower in fat and cholesterol," Merry argued.

He noticed Cait actually smiling.

"Low-fat turkey chili," he said to her, crossing his eyes. "Can you believe that, Cait?" He shook his head.

He twirled one of Cait's ponytails like a jump rope, and she didn't pull away from him. A little laugh escaped her throat. Finally, a happy sound from his little girl!

"Gobble…gobble," mocked Ty.

Cait actually giggled. He hadn't heard her do that since her mother had left.

Wanting to share his happiness with Merry, he looked over at her and noticed she wasn't laughing with them. Her shoulders were slumped and her eyes were lowered. He hadn't meant to hurt her feelings— it was all for Cait's sake.

But damn, *turkey* chili?

He had the urge to get Merry away from all this Hollywood stuff and talk to her in private. He wanted to thank her for all she had been doing for Cait, and to tell her that he was only joking about her food.

He needed to sit for a while on the bank of the Rattlesnake. That's where he did his best thinking.

He looked at Caitlin. Whatever light had entered her eyes was now gone. She'd withdrawn once again.

His gut churned and he excused himself from the table. He walked into the barn and saddled Bandit.

As far as he was concerned, he had done all the modeling that he was going to.

Chapter Eight

He'd just mounted Bandit when Merry walked into the barn. "Buck?"

"Yeah?"

"I didn't think about the turkey. I—I—"

"Don't apologize. I was kidding. Cait made a little noise like she was going to laugh, and I hoped to get more out of her. She actually smiled, Merry. That meant a lot to me, but I'm sorry it was at your expense." Bandit walked closer to Merry, and Buck reined him back. "Hey, do they need you anymore?"

"I guess we're done."

He kicked off a stirrup, leaned over and offered his hand to Merry.

She hesitated, confused, but he could tell the exact

second when she understood what he couldn't form into words.

She put her foot in the stirrup, and he swung her up behind him.

Her arms went around him naturally and he could hear her heavy breathing. This was no doubt her first time on a horse, and she probably was scared.

"Relax, Merry," he said. "Just relax. I won't let you fall. Put your arms around me and hold on."

He nudged Bandit forward, out the barn door and over to the table where everyone was still sitting. "Ty, would you mind keeping an eye on Caitlin?"

Ty raised both eyebrows. "Sure. No problem, big brother."

He noticed Cookie grinning. Some of the other boys whistled. Joanne, Merry's publicist, looked mortified. Tim grabbed his camera and started flashing. Buzz had his movie camera trained on them.

Buck trotted the big horse for a while, then slowed him down to a walk. Neither he nor Merry said a word until they reached the bank of the Rattlesnake.

He could have gone on forever with Merry's arms around his waist and her breasts pressing against his back. She was as stiff as steel at first, but he could tell when she finally started to relax and enjoy the ride.

A few days ago, he had wanted nothing more than to put her back on the plane to Boston. Now he was thinking that he wanted her to stay awhile.

"Whoa, Bandit," he said.

The horse stopped and immediately dipped his head

to the thick green grass along the riverbank. Bandit liked it here as much as he did.

Buck never tired of the glittering river that snaked through the ranch. It was his little oasis in the desert. A place where he could just lie in the sweet-smelling grass and watch the clouds go by. A place where he had fond memories of a happy, carefree childhood spent with his family.

Yet it was a place where his dreams never materialized. He'd always dreamed of building a place of his own by the river. He'd wanted to see a half dozen of his kids fish and swim in the sparkling, clear water; ride their horses and laugh like kids should.

But it just wasn't in the cards for him.

Twisting in the saddle, he was just about to help Merry off, when she mumbled, "I can do it," and proceeded to fall in a heap on the ground.

Quickly, he swung off Bandit to help her up. "Shoot, Merry. Why didn't you wait for me? Are you hurt?" He ran his hands over her ankles.

"I'm perfectly fine," she said. "It's not your fault, my butt fell asleep, and I think my legs did, too. Just give me a minute."

Her khaki pants were stained from the grass and her pretty pink blouse was wrinkled. She'd lost a sandal, and her golden hair was mussed.

She was still the most beautiful woman he'd ever seen.

She pulled her hands up from the grass and looked around. "Are there snakes around here?"

"If there are, we probably scared them off by now."

That seemed to satisfy Merry, probably until she had time to think about it.

"What a gorgeous setting," she said, looking out at the river.

"This is one of my favorite spots on the ranch. I come here to think. I'd miss it like hell if I had to sell it for a golf course and condos or whatever Russ Pardee, my less-than-neighborly neighbor, wants to do with it."

He helped her up. She was still wobbly, so it seemed natural to wrap his arms around her and hold her close.

She smelled of expensive perfume, coconut shampoo and fresh air. He looked down into her emerald eyes and at her perfect lips. He wanted to kiss her, to taste her.

So he did.

His lips met hers, gently at first. Then when Merry seemed willing, he deepened the kiss. Her lips parted with a soft moan. He heard her sharp intake of breath, then she leaned into him, running her fingers through his hair, knocking his hat off.

He kissed her again, harder, slanting his mouth against hers. He felt like he just found an oasis in the desert, a lifeline in a storm. His body hummed with the long-forgotten feelings of a sexual rush, and he wanted more—much more.

"Buck," she breathed, but it seemed more like a warning, instead of consent. Her eyes fluttered open, and she looked ready to bolt.

He knew the moment was over. She had come to her senses and remembered that he was a cattle rancher and not someone who ran in her society circle.

Try as he might, Buck couldn't see Merry ever being happy on the ranch.

He wasn't stupid. There was no doubt in his mind that Merry would bolt like the other females he fell for. It was just as well she'd stopped him, or he would have made love to her right on the bank of the river.

She looked at him as if she wanted to say something, then turned and walked toward the water, ever watchful for snakes or whatever else she might want to be rid of, including a long, tall cowboy from the Rattlesnake Ranch.

Buck's kisses sent Merry's senses to heaven and back, and if her heart rate didn't calm, she was going to have a heart attack right here and now and tumble into the sparkling river. Her body would float clear down to Mexico. No doubt Joanne would think of an attention-getting press release: Meredith Bingham Turner Accidentally Falls Into River While Picking Southwestern Herbs For a Special Dish.

No other man's kisses had affected her like Buck's just had. The power of her reaction shocked her. She was shaking and she could hardly stand, could still taste him on her lips. In another second she would have been tearing at his clothes to touch his warm, tanned skin. In spite of everything she'd said about not getting involved with men, she'd wanted him.

But why was she so attracted to Buck?

Maybe it was because he didn't seem to want anything from her, at least not that she could tell. Actually, he wanted her to go home and not touch his ranch.

But what did she really know about him? She knew he cared for his siblings. He worked hard and was very proud of his ranch. She liked the way she filled out his jeans—and how he had looked with his shirt off. She liked his sense of humor, how he kept trying to win over Cait. She liked a lot of things about him.

And Merry knew she would have found out a lot more if she'd let their kisses run their natural course.

She wanted him.

But she couldn't have him.

She had to constantly worry about the press, more now than ever. Right now her publicity machine was cranking out stories to deflect the George situation. She'd seem too flighty if she were photographed with yet another man.

She couldn't deny that she was attracted to Buck, but she was realistic enough to know they had no future together. She had a job to do and a business to run.

He belonged in the rugged, untamed desert.

She belonged in Boston.

She walked over to where he was sitting, and he looked up but didn't smile.

"I shouldn't have kissed you."

She had thought that she'd be the one to regret their kisses, but she didn't. It saddened her that he did.

"Why not?" she asked.

He hesitated, then answered slowly, as if he were trying to come up with a suitable explanation. "You're a good friend of my sister, and I don't want you to think that it could lead to anything more."

"More?"

"Like anything long-term, if that's what you're

looking for. We're just too different, and you'll be going back to Boston soon and your TV show and all."

"That didn't seem to bother you a minute ago."

"Didn't think of it a minute ago. I had other things on my mind."

"Like what?"

"The ranch, Caitlin, Karen, bills, wondering if I should sell this parcel or not—the usual things I think about. And you."

"So now I'm complicating things more?" she asked, holding her breath. "Why?"

"Because I want to make love to you."

She let her breath out in a big sigh.

"And I think you want the same thing," he added. "Am I wrong?"

She sat down next to him and stared at the glittering water going by. "That's complicated to answer."

"So, I'm complicating things for you, too?"

How could she answer him? He was right. She did want to make love with him. She'd been hot for him ever since she saw him riding toward her on Bandit. But there was her image to consider and the fact that she'd be leaving soon. They were worlds apart—Boston and Lizard Rock.

She wasn't the type to sleep around, either, no matter what the press thought.

His blue eyes looked up at her, and she couldn't help thinking of what a physical relationship with Buck would be like. Would he kiss and tell, too?

Buck certainly wasn't like that. Then again, that's what she'd thought about George Lynch.

Would she ever trust anyone again?

Her emotions were churning. There was something about Buck—something warm and kind, yet battered and bruised. He was trying to push on in spite of the obstacles that were thrown in his path. In that way, they were two of a kind.

"I think it's better that we don't get involved," she finally said.

"You can't deny that you aren't interested in me."

"I—I—" Feeling her cheeks flame, she just couldn't admit how attracted she was to him. "Don't flatter yourself, Bucklin Floyd Porter."

He raised an eyebrow. "I must have misunderstood your interest, then."

No. You didn't.

"Back in Boston a man wouldn't be as blunt as you. There'd be flowers and dates and some flirting and then…"

"And then he'd finally get you into bed. We don't have the time for all that. If you're willing, let's cut right to the best part with no strings attached."

He smiled. It was a charming smile, a mischievous smile. When he added a wink, she decided he was kidding, just like he was about the turkey chili.

He held out his hand to her, and she took it and sat next to him on the grass.

"Buck, it was just a couple of kisses. It was no big deal."

He put a hand over his heart. "Ouch. That's a blow to my masculinity."

She chuckled. "I didn't mean it that way."

"So let's change the subject." He pointed toward her feet and her sexy sandals. "I'd like you to wear cowboy boots around here instead of those little leather things. It's for your own safety."

She should be flattered that he cared, but he was probably worried that Karen would kill him if she died from a snake bite.

"I don't have any cowboy boots."

"On our way to the hospital tonight, I'll take you to the feed store. They sell boots."

She had to laugh. She couldn't help herself. Shopping for boots at a feed store? What a far cry from Boston.

"I know it's not what you're used to, but—"

She laid a hand on his arm, and felt him tense, so she removed it quickly. "You're right. It's not what I'm used to, but that's okay."

"But this is—"

"The desert. I know."

She looked around at the beautiful landscape, ripe with wildflowers. It was so different from the cement and high-rises of Boston. "Buck, tell me what it was like living on the ranch and having a large family."

He nodded, then focused on the glittering river meandering by as if he were going back in time.

"It was wonderful—everything a kid would want. Horses to ride, tractors to drive, roundups in the spring. What exactly do you want to know?"

"Whatever you want to tell me."

He leaned back on his elbows. "We all worked hard together, but there was always time for fun. We each got a pony of our own when we were old enough to sit in the saddle. My grandfather insisted on it. Gramps lived with us for a long time after my grandmother died. He was quite the character."

"That must have been fun. I never knew my grandparents."

"He gave me a Harley Panhead when I turned sixteen. It was the best present I ever received, bar none. Every day after school, I rushed through my chores. Then I'd hop on it and tear up the desert until the bell rang for supper."

"Do you still have it?"

"It's in the barn. It's a classic machine now, and it's worth a nice chunk of change. I haven't had time for it in a month of Sundays, but yet I can't stand the thought of selling it."

She could hear the disappointment in his voice, but understood his situation. She hadn't had time for fun in ages, either.

"One day Gramps came back from the doctor. He was diagnosed with liver cancer, but I didn't know that until later. He told me to go and saddle up our horses, so I did. Gramps took me all the way up to Lizard Rock then pointed down at this valley. The ranch was only a speck, and I could see the Rattlesnake River winding its way across the land—Porter land."

Buck's voice trailed off to a whisper, and he sat upright, staring up at the mountain in the distance.

"'The land is your legacy, boy. Don't ever forget that,' Gramps said. 'It's been in our family since after the Civil War. I want you to take care of it, Bucklin. Don't let me down. Hear, boy?'"

"You were named after your grandfather," Merry guessed, feeling closer to him at this moment than any man she'd ever known.

He nodded, looking off at Lizard Rock in the distance.

"And that's why you've always taken care of the ranch?" she asked. "Because of what your grandfather said?"

Buck nodded. "But my dad felt the same way about the ranch, and we all got the same lecture from him. So after my folks died, it went to all of us. I was in the army and got a hardship discharge to come home. Karen was sixteen. Ty and Lou were just kids."

"And you mostly raised Karen, Ty and Louise and took care of the ranch and sent them to college," she added, remembering that Karen had told her that during their first day of freshman year. Karen had opened a bottle of tequila and they became best friends after one shot.

Karen had confessed on more than one occasion that she felt guilty leaving Buck with the younger two, but he'd insisted that she go to college. He believed very strongly in education.

But Buck hadn't gone to college. He had stayed on the ranch and raised his siblings.

"Ty and Lou were a great help around the ranch. Even though they were young, they did as much as they could. They were good kids. I don't know what I would have done without Karen, either. I was just so damned glad to be back home. I missed the ranch when I was in the army and thought of it every day."

Merry remembered that his parents had died in a car accident in Florida on the way to a friend's wedding.

"The beef market changed one day. Prices fell. Things got bad. With the current economy, and various mad-cow scares and whatnot, they've gotten much worse."

"And now you have to resort to making it into a dude ranch."

He didn't answer. He didn't have to. She understood it all so clearly now.

"This is Porter land. Porters have lived and died here. Porters will always live here. And that'll never change as long as I'm still breathing."

"And I'm the one changing it—making turkey chili and bringing in a camera crew and a photographer. Sleeping in your room and making myself at home in your mother's kitchen."

"You're here at the invitation of my sister. I'm trying to think of you as her guest, not someone who's going to change the ranch house, but I have to tell you that it's been damn difficult."

"Buck, didn't you tell them you didn't want a dude ranch?"

"I sure the hell did, but I was outvoted. The bills were mounting, and I was going under. I wanted to diversify into rodeo-stock contracting. But the banks turned me down, so Ty and the girls came up with the dude-ranch plan."

"I see."

"I can't blame them if they want the ranch to be bringing in some money. I want that, too, but not by running a damn hotel."

Merry *definitely* understood him now.

"I can't help but feel that I've disappointed generations of Porters. Truth be told, any profit from the dude ranch will barely touch all the debt, not for a long time. So, I feel like it's a lot of change for nothing."

"You underestimate Karen and me. With her business background, my experience and my name, well, I can promise you that it'll be big."

He slowly shook his head.

"Let me just say that you've carried a heavy weight for a lot of years." Her heart pounded and she felt a familiar anger building up inside her. "Why do relatives do that? They make unrealistic demands that their children struggle to carry out, and then they feel like failures when they cannot live up to their parents' expectations." She shot the words out like bullets.

"Sounds like you've been down the same trail as I have."

His pitch-black hair blew around his face in the slight breeze, and Merry wanted nothing more than to run her fingers through its silky length.

"I can't live up to my parents' expectations, either." There it was out, she'd told him point-blank. "I never get their approval or a damn compliment. So I gave up trying. It's easier that way."

He took her hand. "I already figured that out from the conversation with your mother at the hospital. We're quite the pair, aren't we?"

"Guilt, obligation, trying to please…does it get any worse than that?"

"Well, in my case, throw in an ex-girlfriend and an ex-wife who left me for better offers."

"In my case, throw in a couple of serious boyfriends who used me and my money than blabbed to the tabloids."

Buck put his arm around Merry and pulled her to his side.

"Now, if we had a pitcher of beer and there was a done-me-wrong song playing on the jukebox, we'd be all set."

"We could cry in our beer," Merry added, smiling. "But I'd rather just turn my lawyers loose on them."

Buck played with her fingers. "I wasn't very nice to you when you first arrived. Please understand...I just don't want my home changed. I don't want it all dressed up and decorated with ruffles and bows and doilies and silver tea sets and flowers sticking out of bleached cow skulls, and stuff like that. I don't want strangers in my home, in our home."

He stood up, walked to where she had dispatched his hat during their kiss, and put it back on. Obviously, that was all he was going to say on the topic, and the expression on his face reflected that he shouldn't have said as much as he did.

Merry followed him. "Buck, why do you think I'm going to dress up the ranch with ruffles and bows and all that?"

He shrugged. "Karen said that you'd help set up a couple of places in New Hampshire and Vermont."

"Those were bed-and-breakfast inns, and because they were in Vermont and New Hampshire, I decorated them in the country style. B and B's are the staple crop of hospitality in New England. Not in Arizona." She gave a little chuckle.

"Well, that's good."

"Let me just ease your mind a bit more." She put a hand on his arm. "As soon as you all give me the word, I'll stop the wheels from turning and head back home, but until then I promised Karen to make it a success and I can't let her down. I won't let her down. And I won't let you down, either."

He nodded and stared out at the water again, his hands clenched into tight fists. "I have another plan that I'm working on, too."

"Good. Anything I can help with?"

"No. It's something that I have to do myself."

"Will it work?"

"Don't know yet."

"Why don't I just loan you the money to get out of debt so you can buy the rodeo animals and whatever else you want?"

He looked as if he was just stung by a scorpion. "No."

"I'll *give* you the money, then. Whatever you want."

"No." His eyes darkened, like thunderclouds before a storm. "I won't take your money, and please don't offer again."

"I didn't mean to insult you, Buck, but—"

"I'm not one of those guys who'd use you for your money like—"

"George. He's the most recent one."

"I'm not like him. I don't want your money."

She took a deep breath, looked deep into his eyes, and decided that if he were setting her up, she'd drag him through the cacti behind her gray rental car all the way to Texas.

"Listen, Buck…"

"We didn't ask you for money. So thanks, but no thanks. As I said, I have a plan, but things are not ready yet."

His stock had just gone up several notches in her book.

"Until I hear otherwise, I promise no ranch dressing." She chuckled at her play on words. "No ruffles. No bows. Your house feels like a home to me. It's perfect the way it is. There's history in it—the history of a warm, loving family. I love your mother's paintings and her dishes. I love every piece of that gorgeous furniture. I love the tree bed that I'm sleeping in that almost looks like it's blooming. And in spite of the fact that I'm scared that every twig is a snake and every dark spot is a tarantula, this is the some of the most beautiful country I have ever seen, and I've been all over the world."

He took in every inch of her face. It was almost as if he was seeing her in a new light.

"Glad to hear that." He raised an eyebrow. "So you like the tree bed?"

"It's incredible—magnificent. An artist made that piece. Do you know who—"

In spite of their vows not to get involved, he reached for her, pulled her into his arms and kissed her again. Merry gently held his face in her hands, matching his passion.

Just one last kiss….

Chapter Nine

When they arrived back at the ranch, Buck swung off Bandit and then helped Merry down.

Merry hurried away from him before Joanne picked up on any vibes between her and Buck.

And there were definite vibes, at least on Merry's end.

"Shall we wrap everything up?" Merry asked, sneaking a peak at Buck, but he'd already disappeared into the barn, leading Bandit.

"We already wrapped," Joanne said, eyeing Merry's wrinkled, grass-stained clothes. "A cowboy, Meredith?"

Merry took her arm and pulled her farther away from the barn. "You're overstepping your bounds, Joanne. My personal life isn't anyone's business."

"I beg to differ. You hired me to deflect bad publicity. Bad publicity can affect your corporation."

"I *am* my corporation." Merry crossed her arms. "And I'm tired of being manipulated."

"Merry, listen to me." She looked up to the sky as if she were praying for patience. "Your fans think of you as Miss Hospitality, the best hostess in the world, a great cook, heir to Martha Stewart's throne. You've been billed as the perfect woman. Your fans don't want you sleeping around with cowboys." She snapped her gum. "Let me put it this way, he's just another George Lynch."

Merry's cheeks heated, and she spoke through gritted teeth, "Buck's not like that, and I'm not sleeping with him."

"But you will. You're a sucker for guys like him. I did some checking, and he's in debt up to the dent in his cowboy hat."

"I already know that." Merry was getting tired of this conversation, tired of everything. "That's why I'm here."

"Has he asked you for money yet?"

No. I offered it.

"He's not that type," Merry said.

"Sure he is. They all are. It's just a matter of time. He's just going to romance you a bit first." Joanne checked her watch. "Well, I'm out of this hellhole. I can't wait to get back to civilization and culture."

Even though Merry wanted to fire her on the spot, she couldn't. Joanne was just voicing Merry's own thoughts—and fears—about Buck.

The rest of her staff was loading up the van, and Merry walked over to say goodbye to them.

"Thank you," she said. "Overnight me the pictures and the tape as soon as they're ready." She waved as they drove away.

A feeling of relief came over her. Getting rid of Joanne was like the joy of tossing out a tin of factory-made Christmas fruitcake.

Buck walked toward her as soon as they were gone. "I'm going to take a quick shower. Then I figure we can head to town and shop for your boots, grab a bite to eat and visit Karen."

"Sounds good. I'll be ready in an hour."

"Make it a half hour. I think the feed store closes at five."

"Okay."

"Do you mind if we take Caitlin?" Buck asked. "I think Ty deserves a break."

"No. Certainly not."

"Would you tell her to get ready?"

"Sure."

Merry watched him as he strode to the bunkhouse. He had a great walk and a great butt. She could have watched him walk all day.

She thought of his kisses at the river and became hot all over again. "It's just the desert," she mumbled as she hurried up the stairs into the house.

She was going to take a shower herself—a cool shower.

"Caitlin?" she shouted from the living room. "Cait?"

When she walked into the kitchen, she noticed Cait

making hats out of paper napkins. There had to be two dozen napkins folded.

Ty was on the phone. He gave Merry a wave, then went back to his conversation.

Merry put her hands on Cait's shoulders. "Sweetie, your dad asked me to tell you to get ready. We're going to the hospital to visit your aunt Karen and to get a pair of cowboy boots for me. Okay with you?"

She got up out of her chair, stacked up some hats in a pile, and put them carefully into a paper bag that was on the table.

"Are those for Aunt Karen?"

She nodded.

"She's going to love them," Merry added. "That's a nice present."

The girl left the room with her gift.

"Tell my sister I'll be up later to see her," Ty said to Merry.

"Sure."

Merry was ready with a few minutes to spare. She had taken a quick shower, shampooed her hair and slipped into white slacks and a light-blue blouse.

Walking out to the front porch, she found Caitlin sitting on a chair on the porch with the bag for Karen on her lap.

"Can I join you?" Merry asked. She didn't wait for a response and sat down. She let her hair dry for a few seconds in the sun, then brushed it into a ponytail and tied it back with a string of leather she'd found on Buck's dresser.

"Cait, do you want me to brush your hair and put it into ponytails?"

Cait looked up at her and gave a slight nod.

"Would you get me some rubber bands?"

The girl stood and went into the house. When she returned, she handed Merry two rubber bands, two yellow ribbons and a brush.

"These ribbons will look really pretty with your outfit," Merry said. "Sit here."

The girl sat in front of her on the porch step as she had before. "You have beautiful hair, Cait. Nice and soft. Oh, some tangles here. Hang on. I'll try not to hurt you."

Merry could see the light-blond peach fuzz on the girl's neck. She sat with her hands folded together, waiting patiently for Merry to finish tugging at tangles and fussing with her hair. Merry wished she'd squirm and yell like a normal kid.

"This should be fun tonight. Now, I'm counting on you to help me pick out some boots. I've never worn cowboy boots, so I could really use your help. Okay?"

Merry could have sworn that she heard a hint of a whisper from the little girl.

Buck pulled up in front of the ranch house and couldn't believe his eyes. Caitlin was giving Merry a hug. The girl's eyes were closed and she had a look of contentment on her face. Merry did, too.

If only Merry could somehow reach his daughter, get her to talk.

That was too much to hope for. There wasn't enough time. Merry would be going back to Boston. He ought to make that clear to Cait and make absolutely sure that she understood. He didn't want her becoming too attached to Merry or think it was her fault when it came time for Merry to leave.

He got out of the truck and opened the passenger's side. "Your chariot awaits, ladies."

Merry turned to Cait. "The last time I walked down these stairs in these shoes, a little lizard ran across my foot. I hope that doesn't happen again. Um...uh... You go first, Cait."

Merry's voice was laced with humor, and she was exaggerating her fear. Buck chuckled. Humor and teasing seemed to reach Cait the most. Merry must have figured that out.

Cait laughed and his heart did a little leap in his chest.

Damn if Cait didn't take Merry's hand and lead her down the stairs, as Merry said, "Eeewww" with a hand over her eyes.

Cait laughed again.

He grinned. It felt so damn good to see Cait reacting.

Taking the advice of her psychiatrists, Buck forced himself to calm down and make like it was no big deal.

Cait climbed up into the truck. Before Merry got in, Buck turned and whispered in her ear, "Thank you from the bottom of my heart."

His lips brushed the warmth of her neck. He could smell the scent of roses and maybe vanilla.

Merry gave a slight shudder. "I'm not doing anything special."

"You sure are."

She turned slightly and their lips were merely inches

apart. He wanted to pull her into his arms, to taste her, to touch her.

But his daughter was watching them.

As he walked around to the driver's side, he felt some of the concrete in his gut begin to crack. He dared not to hope for too much, yet he couldn't help himself. He wanted a miracle.

If that miracle came in the form of a TV cook and hospitality expert from Boston, then so be it.

To think he'd never wanted her to come in the first place. Now he didn't want her to go.

Not just yet.

As they sat in the truck with Cait between them, Buck kept glancing at Merry. "You look different," he finally said.

"I didn't put any makeup on."

"You don't need it."

Smiling at his comment, she looked out the window at the scenery. She remembered that when she'd first arrived, she'd thought that the saguaros were ominous and foreboding. Now she was used to them and they looked majestic and strong with their arms reaching up to the sky.

"I told you about my younger days on the ranch. Now you tell Cait and me what it was like growing up in Boston," Buck said.

"Well, I'm an only child." She put a hand over Cait's. "Like Cait." Merry didn't want to talk over the girl's head as if she wasn't even there. "My parents are stockbrokers. They have their own business. Turner Brokerage."

Buck nodded.

"When I was growing up, they were busy building up their company and making social contacts—that kind of thing. Luckily I had Pamela." She smiled at Cait, who seemed to be listening. "You would have loved Pam. She's just like your aunt Karen."

"Was she a relative?" Buck asked.

"No. She was the housekeeper, cook, my friend and the parents I didn't have all rolled into one. She was the one who taught me to cook and to enjoy decorating and baking. Pam was the reason why I went into the hospitality and culinary programs at Johnson & Wales University in Rhode Island." She turned her attention to Cait. "That's where I met your aunt Karen. She was taking the business program."

"Where's Pam now?" he asked.

"She's living with her sister in Connecticut, but I see her whenever I can, which isn't often enough. I just adore her." She patted Princess's head. "Pam was the one who gave me Bonita, my stuffed cat, when I was a child."

"And how did you get on TV?" Buck asked.

"With hard work and some help from a teacher at J & W who thought I had potential."

"Do you like what you're doing?" he asked.

"I used to, but somehow it all got too big and out of hand. Sometimes I feel like I've lost control of my company," she finally confessed, blurting out things that had been hiding in the back of her mind. "I don't enjoy what I've become."

"What's that?"

"A conglomerate." Merry sighed. "I've lost the fun. I've lost control."

"It's your life and it's your business. Take back control, Merry, and trim it down so you're doing what you want. Then maybe the fun will return."

"Do you think it's that simple?"

He shrugged. "It's probably easier said than done. I want to diversify, and here I'm advising you to cut back. What's more important is what *you* think."

"I think you are probably right," she said, brushing some stray hair back from Cait's face. "If only it was that easy. Huh, Cait?"

Cait shrugged and closed her eyes. Merry put her arm around Cait's slim shoulders and moved the girl to rest against her side. Cait didn't protest or move away.

Merry knew that she'd miss Cait when she was gone. She was like a little lost soul, a lonely girl who couldn't reach out, who tried to steel herself from hurt.

In many ways, Cait reminded Merry of herself.

Merry loved the feed store. It was like a Wal-Mart but with twice as much stuff packed into a tenth of the space.

The owner of the Lizard Rock Feed and Hardware, Dan Hollister, recognized her immediately and told her right off that he didn't miss any of her shows.

He said that he'd owned the store since Buck was in diapers, then proceeded to show her a fascinating cooking kit where two metal plates and two metal mugs were contained in a frying pan bottom and a Dutch oven, complete with lid, and all screwed together with the handle of the frying pan.

Merry inspected every inch. "Fascinating. I love this."

"Dan, Merry needs a pair of nice, comfortable cowboy boots," Buck said.

"You know where they are, Buck. I'm enjoying the lady's company."

"But I need the lady's feet over here."

Dan pushed his glasses up on his nose. "I guess that's the truth." He turned to Merry. "Go ahead, miss. Buck's in some awful hurry. It used to be that a man could talk to his customers."

The smell of leather and beeswax permeated the store and the wooden floor under her creaked. She wished she had more time to explore. All kinds of interesting things could probably be found in its nooks and crannies.

Merry scanned the selection of boots in her size. "What kind of boots should I buy?"

"Those black ones over there." Buck pointed to the ugliest boots in the lineup. "They'll do fine. You can wear them around the ranch, and go boot scootin' at the honky-tonk with them at night."

"Boot scootin' at the honky-tonk? Now, there's something I've never done."

"Then you've missed a great part of our culture."

"Indeed I have." She drew out the words. "And do you scoot your boots often?"

"Often enough. I'll take you dancing before you leave."

She didn't think that would be a good idea. She was sure she couldn't boot-scoot to save her life. Ah...but what would it be like to dance with Buck?

Cait pointed to a pair of turquoise boots with a big green saguaro on the side with a wolf howling up at the moon under the cactus. They screamed "tourist," which, of course, Merry was.

"You know, Cait, I like those. They're perfect. I'll try them on," she said.

Buck took the boots off the shelf. "Okay. Sit down."

Merry sat down on one of the two chairs. Cait sat on the edge of a smaller chair.

Buck squatted down in front of her, picked up her foot and slid her sandals off. Her foot looked so tiny in his big hand, and she could feel his calluses under the pad of her foot.

"You should wear socks with boots." He looked around but didn't find what he wanted. "Hey, Dan," he yelled. "Throw me a pair of boot socks for Merry."

In seconds, the socks came flying overhead, and Buck caught them in one hand. Merry felt a tingle down her spine as he pulled her pant leg up and his warm knuckles grazed the length of her leg. She held her breath.

She watched his arm muscles bunch and his shirt pull taut across his strong, wide back as he bent over. She picked up the lid of the shoe box and traced the edge to give her hands something to do, so she wouldn't be tempted to feel Buck's muscles moving under her palms. She stared at the tanned skin at the vee of his shirt as she felt his hands on her legs, pulling up the thick white socks, then the colorful boots.

"Okay. Walk in them."

His voice was hoarse. Maybe he was just as bothered as she was.

When his blue eyes gazed up at her, she had to fight the urge to tell him to take the boots off and put them on again.

"Merry? Do they feel okay?"

She snapped back to life and took a few tentative steps. Surprisingly, they were more comfortable than they had looked. "They feel fine."

"Good. You can wear them now."

A fluffy gray-and-white cat walked over to Buck and scratched her neck on Buck's jeans. He reached down to give the cat a scratch behind the ears. Merry saw Cait wiggle in her seat. Buck must have noticed it, too.

"Do you want to pet the cat?" Buck asked her.

Cait's hand reached out as Buck scooped up the cat and held it in front of her. "Scratch her behind the ears. That's it. She likes that."

Dan called Buck's name.

"Be right there," he yelled, then turned back to Cait. "Do you want to hold her?"

Cait sat back and held out her arms as Buck gently placed the cat on her lap.

"What's your cat's name, Dan?" Buck asked.

Dan peeked over the display of boots. "That's Ariel."

"The cat's name is Ariel, Caitie." Then he turned to Merry. "I'll be right back."

Merry petted the cat with Caitlin. Every now and then their hands would touch, and Cait would glance up at her.

"She's a pretty cat," Merry said, then spotted a rack of women's jeans. "I'm going to be right over there, Cait, to look at the jeans. Okay?"

Cait's attention didn't waiver from Ariel as Merry

looked at the selection in her size. She didn't mean to overhear Dan talking to Buck.

"Sorry, Buck, but your account is way up there and way overdue. I wish things were different, but times are tough for us all and—"

Buck held his hand up. "I understand, Dan." Merry peeked over the counter and could see Buck emptying his wallet. "Will this do for now? I'll work on the rest as soon as I can."

"Sure."

She was hurting for Buck. It must be embarrassing for him.

A look at Dan told her that he was just as miserable.

She hurried back to Cait's side. The cat was in her glory, and so was Cait.

"Ready, ladies?" When Buck returned to them, he wasn't the same happy man. "Cait, honey, we have to go now."

Cait lifted her hands from the cat, and it ran off. Cait stood and followed them to the front of the store. Merry reached for her wallet and pulled out two hundred-dollar bills for the boots and socks. Dan gave her change and put her sandals in the empty box and slipped the box into a bag.

"Come again, Miss Turner."

"I will. You have an interesting store here."

Dan beamed, then gave Buck an uneasy smile. "See you soon, Buck?"

Buck nodded. "Soon."

He turned on his heels and held the door open for them to exit the store.

On the sidewalk, Merry turned to Buck. "Let's eat before we see Karen. I'm famished."

Then she realized that Buck had probably just given Dan all his money. She didn't expect him to pay, for heaven's sake, but she could tell he was the type of man who'd insist on it.

"I'd like to treat my host and hostess for dinner, to thank you for giving me the royal treatment."

Buck opened his mouth to protest, but Merry held up her hand. "If you'd ever watched my TV show, you'd know that's the proper thing to do."

He thought for a while, looking as if he was going to say no.

"Don't argue with me, cowboy. I'm dying for real Mexican food, so let's go."

"I know just the place for Mex," he finally said. "We can walk there."

He took Merry's hand and it seemed like a natural thing, as if they had walked hand in hand many times before. He offered his other hand to Caitlin, but she didn't take it. Instead she walked to Merry's side and took her hand instead.

Even in the dim light, she could see the hurt in Buck's eyes. The man wasn't having a good evening.

"Look at that sky," she said in awe, hoping to help Buck think of something different.

It was a beautiful sunset, one that she'd always remember. The setting sun cut vivid streaks of orange and red in the sky, and it was the perfect night for a walk. A warm breeze whispered around them, and

Merry took a deep breath of the fresh air. Their boots thumped on the sidewalk and it made her smile.

She'd never felt better in her life. She was makeup-less, her hair was in a ponytail and she was wearing turquoise cowboy boots with big saguaros and wolves on them. She was with the handsomest man in the world and the sweetest little girl.

She thought of the incident at the feed store and it dampened her good mood. A man like Dan would let Buck owe him a fortune, before he called in the loan.

"This is it. Casa Juanita." Buck opened the door for her and she took a deep whiff of the delicious smells.

A beautiful young woman in tight white jeans and a red halter top headed right for Buck. She stood on her toes, cupped his face in her hands and kissed him full on the lips. He grinned down at the woman and said something in Spanish. Merry heard him call her Juanita as he took her arms from around his neck and stepped back.

Merry knew instantly that they had been lovers. Or maybe they still were.

Another shot of jealousy coursed through Merry at that discovery, and she barely nibbled at the delicious chicken chimichangas that she'd ordered, especially when Juanita hovered around Buck and touched him at every possible opportunity.

"Meredith?" A patron shouted from the booth across the aisle. "Meredith Bingham Turner? I thought it was you! Can I have your autograph?" Soon the woman was at Merry's side, thrusting a place mat and a pen in front of her.

Merry signed her name and handed everything back, keeping a gracious smile on her face.

She could hear the ripple of noise, the scraping of chairs. All too soon, there was a line down the aisle and around the perimeter of the restaurant. Buck continued eating and every once in a while, he would look at Merry and grin.

Cait was okay. She seemed content to munch on a triangle of chicken quesadilla and shyly observing the people who stopped by their table.

"Merry's almost done, Cait." Buck finished off Merry's chimichangas then the rest of Cait's meal when she pushed it away.

Finally, Buck excused himself to go talk to Juanita.

Merry felt bereft. She'd just wanted to spend a nice evening talking to Buck and Cait. She didn't know how much longer she'd be here in Arizona. When the painters were done, she could get down to her real work for the dude ranch. The rest she could handle back in Boston.

While talking to two elderly fans about her recipe for cookie dip, Merry took the opportunity to pull some money from her purse to take care of the check.

Buck returned a short time later and his eyes settled on the check and the money on the table. Without a word, he picked up the check and the money and handed it to Juanita.

"Sorry, folks," he said to those remaining in line. "But Meredith Bingham Turner has another appointment."

There was a collective groan and then everyone

clapped as Merry stood up. Putting his arm around her, he escorted Merry and Cait out of the restaurant. They had almost made their escape when a woman shouted, "Hey, Merry, is that cowboy your new boyfriend?"

They both turned in the direction of the voice.

"Who's the little girl, Merry?"

Lights flashed. Cameras. She had to get out of there.

She began running outside, dragging Buck and Caitlin along.

Finally, Buck pulled back and shouted, "Whoa. What are you running from?"

"Don't you understand? By midmorning, everyone will know that I had dinner with you and Cait. I wouldn't be surprised if those pictures ended up in some tabloid."

"Is that so bad?"

"We'll be romantically linked."

"The broke cowboy and the rich gal? That's not headline material."

"You're mistaken." She sighed. "It's perfect."

He put his arm around her waist and smiled, then leaned toward her as if he were going to kiss her. "Shall we give them something to talk about?"

She pulled away, mortified. "No. Absolutely not."

Buck's smile disappeared as more cameras flashed. He started up his truck and made a U-turn in the road as all his bills slid down the dashboard and fell into Merry's lap.

Chapter Ten

Doc Goodwater extended his hand to Buck. "Your sister can go home the day after tomorrow. I just want to get her eating a little more."

"That's great news. Thanks, Doc." Buck shook his hand, happy that Karen was well enough to leave the hospital. "Thanks for everything."

"That's what I'm here for." The doctor checked his clipboard. "See to it that she gets a lot of rest. I'll have a nutritionist meet with her and prepare some menus."

"No problem." Buck was suddenly glad to have a culinary whiz like Merry at the ranch. She'd know how to cook the right food for his sister.

The doctor paused on his way out, snapped his fingers and turned back. "Buck, there's a horse I'm thinking of buying from Olan Gunderson. I'd like you to take a look at him. It's for my eight-year-old grandson, so he needs to be gentle. I'd appreciate your opinion."

"I'd be glad to. I'll drive out to Gunderson's tomorrow, then give you a call."

"I'll knock a chunk off Karen's bill for your time."

Even though he was feeling like a charity case, Buck kept the smile in position on his face. Did everyone in town know how broke he was?

"That's not necessary, Doc. Matter of fact, I insist that you don't."

Dr. Goodwater nodded, and Buck knew that the man would indeed discount Karen's bill no matter how many times Buck asked him not to.

Buck leaned against the wall outside Karen's room, aware of Karen and Merry talking inside. Karen was still fussing over the pile of napkins that Cait had made into hats.

Cait was standing next to Merry on the side of Karen's bed, and Merry's arm was around her shoulders.

He decided to leave them alone for a while. If he entered the room, Cait would retreat, and his guts always churned when she did that.

He was her father, and his daughter couldn't stand to be near him.

If only Debbie hadn't left like she did.

If only they hadn't fought like they had.

Cait had stopped talking to him the day her mother left. She blamed him, and he didn't have the heart to tell the girl the truth about her mother.

He let out a deep breath as he walked over to the coffee machine. Fishing for two quarters, he punched the button for a cup of black coffee.

It had been an interesting day, starting with the early arrival of Merry's staff. He had to admit, he didn't mind modeling for her. Well, yeah, he minded the modeling, but he didn't mind her watching him.

He rubbed his chin as he watched the coffee pour into the drain of the machine instead of into a cup, which had never appeared.

He drank too much coffee, anyway.

Taking a seat in the waiting room, he stretched out. He remembered how he'd enjoyed the ride to the river with Merry's arms wrapped around his waist. Her cheek was warm against his shirt, and her hair tickled the back of his neck. He could still feel her every breath.

After that it had been quite the night. Picking out boots for Merry and then the conversation with Dan. He owed Dan about twenty grand, and he'd had every intention of paying him back a long time ago, but he hadn't counted on the low beef prices, the barn needing repairs and trying to keep the John Deere alive in addition to all the usual expenses: fence and feed, a payroll to make, tuition due and now Karen's operation, most of which wasn't covered by their crummy, very expensive, insurance.

Buck clamped his hands together when he remembered his conversation with Dan. He knew what he had to do in order to pay off his debt to the man, and he couldn't put it off any longer.

He had to sell the motorcycle that Gramps had given him for his high school graduation.

And he had to make more furniture or else sell some pieces from the house that he'd made for his parents. Remembering how much they both had loved his work, he didn't want to do that, but Karen's surgery and Merry's arrival didn't allow him the time to make much progress on his inventory.

If he believed half of what his old army pal, Jack Brooks, had to say, he'd be able to save the ranch with his work. Jack had planned a gala show and sale of Buck's work at his Scottsdale gallery, and was a well-known and respected artist in his own right. People came from all over to visit him.

"With the kind of furniture you make, you'll make a killing," Jack guaranteed. "I'm going to have a big pre-sale party for my special customers and do a lot of advertising. You'd better be prepared for extra orders, too."

Buck always thought that when he needed money, he'd get it rodeoing, but he couldn't leave Cait to work the circuit. It was bad enough that her mother had left them to become a country singer. Buck didn't want to be away from home that long.

Scottsdale, Arizona—where the rich and famous lived and retired. He sure hoped they liked his furniture as much as Jack thought they would.

Merry was rich and famous, too. He had never actually realized how famous she was, but until he saw the line of fans form at the Mexican restaurant it hadn't sunk in.

Merry had been upset when their picture was taken. Unlike his ex-wife, Debbie, who'd always loved being in front of a camera. Debbie Dalton was everywhere: magazine covers, CD covers, posters. A few weeks ago, she'd even had her own special on Country Music Television, which he'd watched in the privacy of the barn with a six-pack and a bag of tortilla chips for company.

He didn't feel anything for Debbie anymore. But he couldn't regret marrying her, either. After all, she'd given him Caitlin.

They'd rarely made love after Cait was born. Debbie was afraid of getting pregnant again and not being able to get into her size zero jeans.

He raked his fingers through his hair. What was Cait thinking? Was she still hoping that Debbie would come back and be a mother to her? What horrible thing had he done that his little girl wouldn't talk to anyone? Why did she recoil every time he came near her?

He knew Cait was familiar with Merry from watching her on TV, but still there was something more about her that Cait had warmed to.

He heard Merry's laughter down the hall and smiled. "Meredith Something Turner," he mumbled. Her kisses melted his hat, charred his boots and fired up everything in between.

City gal and cowboy.

Successful businesswoman and bankrupt rancher.

Been there. Done that. Never again.

How could he trust another woman with his heart? How could he even consider getting involved with another woman who had drive, ambition and goals beyond anything that he could imagine?

Fame had already stolen one love from him and his

child. There was no way he wanted to put Cait—or himself—into the same situation.

"A penny for your thoughts," Merry said, startling him.

Buck jumped and looked up. "They're not worth that much. I guess I was just daydreaming. How's my sister?"

He made a move to get up, but she put a hand on his arm to stop him. He felt the heat spread through him as if it were high noon in the desert. Even that little gesture had his body betraying him in spite of what he'd just been thinking—that he needed to stay clear of Meredith Turner.

"Karen's sleeping now. I guess we tired her out, huh, Cait?"

Cait showed no reaction, and Buck swallowed his disappointment. He still hoped for a miracle.

"But Karen loved the napkins hats. Didn't she, Caitie?"

Caitie? He was the only one who called his daughter that.

Cait looked up at Merry and nodded.

"That's nice, sweetheart," Buck said. "And it's good your aunt Karen is sleeping. She needs her rest. Did she tell you that she's coming home on Friday?"

He started toward the elevators, and Merry and Cait walked along with him. He could almost imagine for a second that they were a family.

A notebook appeared in Merry's hand as it always did, and she began writing as she walked. "Yes, she did, and I have a million things to do before she gets home."

Merry scribbled on the pad. "The painters have to wrap up, and her room has to be cleaned and the furniture has to be moved back in place. Curtains need to be washed and hung. I need to buy some groceries for her special diet." She jotted something down after each sentence. "I'll make a meal plan."

"You can't do this all yourself." Buck stopped and looked down at her.

"I certainly can, but I won't. Cait will help me," Merry said, looking down at his daughter. Nonchalantly, she handed Cait her notebook. Cait took it and held it as if she had a newborn baby in her arms. Buck noted that for once, Cait had left Princess, her stuffed cat, in the truck.

Merry gave him a wink and slipped her pen behind an ear. "Well, maybe we can't move that heavy furniture by ourselves."

"Me and the boys will help. It'll be done in no time. And you can make a list of things you need from the store. Cookie can go. He loves to go grocery shopping, and he'd do anything for you," Buck said, hitting the down arrow by the elevator. "So add that to your list—help will be provided. You and Cait can be trail bosses, and we'll do whatever you say."

He held out his hand to her. "Deal?"

Merry's hand glided into his, and they shook on it. He felt a tingling in his gut, and didn't want to let go of her hand.

She turned to Cait. "We're going to enjoy bossing your father around, won't we?"

Merry looked up at him and he noticed a little glint in her eyes—she was flirting with him. He liked that. And he thought it was nice of her to always include Cait in the conversation whenever she could.

Merry furiously wrote in her notebook on the drive back from the hospital to the ranch. Every now and then, she'd pause to ask him a question and then she'd write some more.

He liked how she concentrated on a task. No doubt the house would be perfect after Merry was done, but at least he didn't have to worry anymore that she was going to change things. That was a big relief.

He parked his pickup by the side of the barn, and they got out. "I'm going to check on the horses. Would you like to join me, Merry?"

The question seemed to take her by surprise. "I'd like that."

"Cait, do you want to come, too?"

Cait was already up the steps of the porch and looking at a note taped to the door.

Buck took the steps two at a time and read it aloud. "Cait, your room is ready. Me and the boys moved your stuff back in. Sweet dreams. And happy early birthday. Uncle Ty."

With that, Cait opened the door and went into the house.

The two of them stood on the porch and he could tell by the look on Merry's face that she was feeling sorry for him again. Damn, he didn't want that.

He shrugged. "So, her birthday present won out over the horses. If I were her age, I'd be curious, too."

"Aren't you going to come and see?" Merry asked.

He looked in the direction of the barn and shook his head. "You go ahead."

"I'll only be a minute, Buck," Merry said. "If Cait

doesn't want to come to the barn, I'll help her get ready for bed and stay in the house and watch her. Okay?"

The disappointment settling inside of him burned like campfire coffee. He didn't want to let her go. He could see to the horses and then join her inside, but he didn't want that. He wanted—and needed—to work on his furniture in the barn, and wanted her company while he did it.

He took Merry's hands. "Thanks, but that's not necessary. There's a monitor on Cait's wall. Just turn it on. We'll be able to hear her in the barn."

She stared down at their connected hands, then looked up. She smiled and let out a nervous breath.

She was nervous? Around him?

She nodded and went into the house.

Buck almost ran to the barn. If he hurried with his chores, he could spend more time alone with Merry. But his gait slowed when he remembered a time when Cait would never leave his side, when she would join him at the stalls and talk to the horses in her sweet, singsong voice as she'd pet each one.

Maybe someday his daughter would come back to him.

He heard the intercom click on, and the noise of a car commercial filled the barn. Ty must have given Cait the TV set he'd bought her. He never could wait until her birthday, which wasn't for another month.

Buck could hear Merry talking to Cait, admiring her new present.

Buck filled Bandit's bucket with water, hooked it to the corner of his stall, and absentmindedly reached over to give the big black stallion a pat. He did the same to the other eight horses in the barn.

Just as he finished, he spotted Merry. He'd never even heard her come in.

His boots rooted to the floor as he took her hand, his heart pounding in his chest as if he'd just ridden a bucking bull for eight seconds.

He raised her hand to his lips. He had never done that kind of thing in his life, but he couldn't resist. It felt right. Damn right.

As he gazed down into her emerald eyes, he saw that she was blinking back tears.

"Merry? Did I do something wrong?"

"No." Her voice was a whisper. "You did everything just right, but what's happening between us?"

He squeezed her hand. "I think you know."

"What happens next?" she asked.

"I think you know that, too." His heart started to thump in his chest. He told himself that it'd only be sex, and soon they'd part ways. No strings attached.

"Cait's ready for you to tuck her in."

Well, damned if that didn't throw cold water on his thoughts.

"That was always Karen's job." He shook his head. "Believe me, Cait doesn't want me around."

"That shouldn't stop you." Her green eyes were concerned, sad.

"It has."

"It hurts you when she turns away from you, doesn't it?"

"Yeah."

She took his hand in hers. "Come anyway, Buck."

His mouth went dry. "You don't…uh…" What kind of a father was he to avoid his own daughter? What kind of a *man* was he?

She was feeling sorry for him again. That wasn't what this was all about.

"Merry, it's like hitting your head against a brick wall. It feels good when you stop."

"Don't give up on her. She needs you more than ever."

"It's been almost two years. Two long years."

"But you've seen some reaction from her lately." She squeezed his hand. When tears pooled in her eyes, it made him crazy.

"Ah, don't do that."

"She reminds me…of *me*…when I was her age," Merry said. "She needs you. She's lonely. If her mother isn't around, then you need to compensate for that."

"I've tried. Dammit, I've tried." His voice was hoarse and low, and he could hear his own frustration.

"Don't give up now, Buck. Keep trying."

She put a hand on his cheek, and she smiled up at him. He was falling for this woman, and falling hard. He couldn't be that stupid.

"You're right. Come on," he said. "Let's go tuck my daughter into bed."

As he thought, Caitlin had her new Mickey Mouse TV set on. Cait was sitting on the edge of her bed, not moving, mesmerized by what she was watching.

"Oh…Debbie Dalton," Merry said. "I have her CD. She's marvelous."

Then she heard the sound of Cait's gentle sobbing.

"She's Cait's mother." Buck walked over and shut the TV off. Then he sat down next to Cait on the bed and put an arm around her.

This time she didn't pull away. Instead, she started to cry. Buck pulled her onto his lap and rocked her back and forth.

The scene broke Merry's heart.

Debbie Dalton was Buck's ex-wife? Karen had never told her that, for heaven's sake.

It was all making some kind of sense. Karen had wanted to tell her something at the hospital, but Caitlin had been there on both occasions.

She watched as Buck hugged Cait, watched his little girl cling to him. She sobbed quietly as he smoothed her hair.

"Let it out, honey. Let it out," he said gently, rocking her slowly.

Merry said a silent prayer for both of them, and left the room so father and daughter could be alone.

Merry tried to sleep, she was exhausted, but what she'd just witnessed kept rolling around in her mind.

She thought she'd imagined the knock on the door.

"Merry? Can I come in?"

The thick door creaked open, and Buck stood silhouetted in the hallway light.

She could hear the need in his voice, the pain, the hope. She knew that if she let him in they'd make love. She should tell him to leave, but she couldn't form the words.

"Come in."

"You know what I want, Merry. You should probably tell me to leave. Just say the words."

"I—I can't."

The door clicked behind him. "I need you, Merry. I want you."

She threw back the bed linens, got out and walked toward him. She put her hands in his. "What about Cait?"

"She's sleeping."

She placed a hand on his cheek, and her fingertips felt some wetness at the corner of his eye.

"Cait always freezes when she sees her mother on TV or hears her on the radio, but this time was different." He squeezed Merry's hands. "She cried and she let me hold her. Cait finally cried." His voice was shaky and low. "Her psychiatrists said that might happen. It means that she's had a breakthrough."

Merry nodded. "That's fabulous, Buck. Fabulous."

He pulled her into a tight embrace. "I can't help thinking you had something to do with that."

Her heart did a little flip. She'd like to believe that she had something to do with Cait's breakthrough, but she didn't see how. She ran her palms along his strong biceps, wanting to touch him. "I didn't do anything, Buck."

"Sure you did. Cait knows you care for her—maybe even love her. Right from the beginning she connected with you. I could see it."

"I do love her. She's a wonderful little girl." Merry could smell the sweet scent of hay on him. "Like I said, she's a lot like me when I was her age."

Buck pulled back and looked at Merry, his finger

tracing her lips. Slowly he lowered his head, giving her time to back out. But this was what she'd wanted—what she'd been dreaming of.

His kiss was tentative at first, and then deepened. His tongue traced her lips and she sighed, wanting more.

She could feel every nerve of his body pulsing with desire. He moved his fingertips over her breasts, and then cupped them in his hands.

She didn't protest. Instead her head leaned back, giving him access to her neck. That was all the invitation he needed.

As he noticed her suitcases in the corner, a million things bounced around his brain. The suitcases reminded him that she'd be leaving soon.

The warning signal in his head told him that she was a bigger celebrity than Debbie ever dreamed of being. They had no future together. She wouldn't stay.

Right now, he didn't care. He wanted her.

She looked at the tree bed, then back at him. "I've dreamed of making love with you in this bed."

Music to his ears. "I was dreaming the same dream."

She played with the top button of her nightshirt. "Oh?"

"Since the first day you arrived."

"I don't think so." She chuckled. "You just about told me to go home."

"Maybe...but I still wanted to kiss you." He kissed her forehead.

He made short work of the three buttons. Then he took the hem of her nightgown and pulled it over her head, letting it drop to the floor.

His fingers circled her nipples, and they puckered in response. Soon, his mouth took over where his fingers had been, his tongue making circles, his teeth tugging until her knees had trouble locking in place.

He lifted her off her feet and moved them both to the bed. As he lay down beside her, he continued his delicious assault on her breasts, down her stomach.

"Buck...that feels so good...so very good. But I want to see you, feel you."

The words were just a whisper. Urgently, her hands pulled at the snaps of his shirt.

With one yank, she got rid of the blasted snaps. He chuckled, reveling in the fact that she wanted him as much as he wanted her. He shrugged out of the damn shirt and pulled her toward him, skin to skin, heat to heat.

He couldn't get enough of her lips, her mouth. He loved the feel of her breasts against his chest. He wanted to touch every inch of her with his mouth, to trail kisses on her perfumed skin. Wanted to find out what would make her cry out in pleasure, wanted to feel her touching him...everywhere.

He lifted her up without breaking the kiss, and her legs locked around him. He felt himself getting harder yet as he pressed against her core.

"Take off your underwear," he whispered in her ear.

"You first, cowboy."

He got up from the bed and yanked off his boots. The rest of his clothes soon followed.

By the light of the moon, he could tell that she was watching his every move.

"You're a beautiful man, especially when you're buck naked." She giggled at her play on words. "Get it?"

"I got it. Very funny." He put his hands on his hips and grinned. "And I've been called many things, but *beautiful* isn't one of them."

"Get over here, cowboy."

She slid out of her underwear. When she lay back down on the bed, it was his turn to look at her by the moonlight.

Merry shivered in anticipation. It didn't take long for his fingers to find her core, to make her wet with desire.

As his mouth found hers, she could feel his fingers slide in and out, making her even wetter, hotter. The roughness of his calluses moved along her bottom, lifting her. The sensation made her tingle all over.

He nibbled at her bottom lip, and more heat coursed through her veins. She couldn't get enough of the taste of him, the feel of his hard muscles.

The pace of their caressing increased as their passion escalated. Merry reached between them and cupped him in her hand. He was thick and hard, and she felt him pulse. His tongue mated with hers as her heart thundered in anticipation of feeling the length of him inside her.

"Buck...oh, Buck...I want you."

"Mmm...wait. Stop." He grabbed her wrist and stilled her hand.

She stared at him. "What's wrong?"

"Not a thing." He rolled over and reached for his pants on the floor. He yanked his wallet out of a pocket and pulled out a foil packet, tossing the wallet to the floor. Tearing a corner of the square open with his teeth, he stood and hurriedly unrolled the condom over his hard length.

She thought it was one of the sexiest things she'd ever witnessed.

"Thank you," she said, cupping him again.

His tongue traced a line down her stomach. His fingers lingered in the coarse curls below then parted her again. She was wet and ready for him.

She sighed. "Now. Please." She could barely speak.

He moved on top of her, and she welcomed the weight of him. He kissed her neck, her breasts, moved his tongue in a way that let her know what he intended to do.

She'd never wanted a man so much in her life.

He entered her slowly, letting her stretch to accommodate him. He filled her completely, tightly.

She felt like she was floating, never to return to earth. It felt right, more than right. It was as if she was part of a whole, and yet complete by herself. When he started to move inside her, she met his pace. Their lovemaking was fast, frenzied, until they both cried out their release all too soon.

He moved to the side, pulling her with him, still hard inside her. He buried his face in her hair and nibbled on her ear.

"That wasn't enough," he said. "I don't know if I'll ever get enough of you."

She kissed the tip of his nose. "The night is young."

"We'll take it slower the next time."

Merry could only smile her consent. She was already working on the next time.

Chapter Eleven

Merry got up just before sunrise because a certain cowboy sleeping on the couch was snoring loud enough to cause Lizard Rock to tumble down Lizard Rock Mountain.

Buck had moved to the couch in the early morning light because he didn't want Cait to catch him in Merry's bedroom.

Merry couldn't sleep. The memory of their lovemaking kept rolling like a movie in her mind. Her face heated just thinking about the things they did.

If she was going to work the cowboys like a trail boss all day, she might as well feed them, and feed Buck. After all the exercise she had last night, she was famished, too.

She felt giddy, energized. Other than making love with Buck again, the thing she wanted to do the most was cook. She loved cooking here, cooking for people who appreciated it, who needed a little comfort food.

The third thing that she wanted to do was to find out more about Debbie Dalton.

Soaping her skin, she thought again of her night with Buck. There wasn't an inch of her that remained untouched from his strong yet gentle hands. She broke into song, being careful not to choose a Debbie Dalton song. It was a long time since she'd been this happy and wanted it to last forever.

She toweled off, got dressed and stopped to take a look at Buck sleeping on the couch as she walked to the kitchen.

He was covered in a serape from the waist down. His chest was bare. She remembered splaying her hands across his tanned chest and feeling the hard muscles and warm skin under her palms.

His need took her breath away, yet he was a considerate lover.

To take her mind off him, she hurried into the kitchen to put the coffee on. She got the dough ready for her maple biscuits and made the batter for her buttermilk pancakes. She boiled some potatoes, and when they were done, she ran them under cold water and then diced them up in a pan along with some peppers and onions for fried potatoes. She found a couple of packs of sausage in the freezer and thawed them out in the microwave.

Thank goodness it was beef sausage, and not turkey or pork.

If she stopped to listen, she could still hear Buck's even snoring. He must be exhausted from their workout last night.

She giggled, and Meredith Bingham Turner never giggled.

Merry walked onto the front porch to do what she had always wanted to do—ring the triangle to call everyone to the meal.

It barely made a sound at first, but then she got the hang of it, and let it rip.

She heard laughter behind her, and she knew immediately that it was Buck. When she turned to face him, she saw that his chest and feet were bare, and he was wearing his jeans. The jeans that fit him like a second skin.

He was sexy—and cute. And she blushed again when she remembered what they'd done all through the night, and for most of the morning.

"No one has rung that in years—not since my mother died."

She wanted to sink through the floorboards. "Oh, I'm sorry."

"No. That's okay. Really. It was good to hear it again, but if you're calling the boys, they're moving the cattle to different ground. They won't be in for another couple of hours."

"Oh. I didn't know. I made breakfast."

"It smells delicious. Will it keep?"

"Yes."

As if on cue, Buck's stomach growled, and he grinned sheepishly.

"I'll check on Cait so you can finish dressing and we'll have breakfast outside under the cottonwood tree by the corral. You know, where we took pictures yesterday?"

He looked surprised. "Breakfast outside?"

"I thought you cowboys are used to eating outdoors. Don't you go on trail drives so you can take your pack of cows to Dodge City or something?"

"That would be a herd of cows. Cattle. And the farthest we drive our cattle is to holding pens by the highway, where they are picked up by eighteen-wheelers."

"What happened to the romance of the Old West?"

"I think I showed you that I can be romantic," he said, his deep voice vibrating clear through to her bones. "Matter of fact, I think I showed you a few times."

"Only a few?" She laughed.

He pulled her into his arms, and she laid her cheek against his warm chest. He kissed the top of her head. "No regrets, Merry?"

"No regrets, Buck."

Not for now. But if she stopped to think, she knew that regrets would set in like a thick Boston fog. She didn't want that to happen. Not yet. She just wanted to enjoy the special feeling inside her, for as long as possible.

She had to keep herself occupied or she would think too much. All the reasons why she shouldn't get further involved with Buck Porter would come to her like ideas for new Christmas recipes.

She looked into his eyes and saw that the sparkle had left them. His regrets had set in already.

He let out a deep breath. "I think I'll take a shower now."

After his shower, Buck walked toward the big cottonwood and couldn't believe his eyes. Merry really knew how to serve a meal. His mother's dishes were set on the long picnic table along with some Mexican platters and bowls that he hadn't seen in years. She had found a tablecloth that his mother had hand-painted with their brand—two *R*s back to back.

All this fuss, and it wasn't even for a photo shoot.

He liked the quart canning jar with the bouquet of wildflowers in it and a big, beat-up blue tin coffeepot in the center of the table steaming with the hot brew. He remembered the pot from the times the whole family had camped out at the line shack, and his mother used to hang it over a campfire to boil the coffee.

He saw that she'd set a place for Cait and remembered how his daughter had clung to him last night, crying her eyes out. He'd been praying that it was the breakthrough he'd been waiting for.

He thought of how he made love with Merry. She was one passionate woman. Were the men in Boston idiots? How could they kiss and tell and hurt her so deeply? How could they use her like that?

Yet their betrayals didn't hold her back from his touch. And in the end, he'd probably end up hurting her just the same. If she was looking for a long-term relationship, she was spitting in the wind as far as he was concerned. He wasn't going to compete against the spotlights and cameras for yet another woman. It was a losing battle.

Never again.

Merry sat sipping coffee from a metal mug that matched the coffeepot. When she saw him, she poured him a cup and pushed it over.

"This is mighty fancy," Buck said. He felt content and comfortable with the homey outdoor scene.

She smiled. "I hope you don't mind that I used what I found in the kitchen."

"I don't mind at all. We never get this fancy. There's nothing like paper plates."

She rolled her eyes. "Normally, I'd tell my guests to eat before things got cold, but things could stay hot for hours outside. It's the desert, you know."

Buck grinned as she shot his own words at him. "Just what I'd say."

"I know." The slight breeze moved her hair, and she tucked a lock behind her ear. "Is Cait still sleeping?"

He nodded, eying the stacks of pancakes under a glass-domed tray. "Yes. She's still out, clutching her stuffed cat."

"How come she doesn't have a real cat? No dog for her, either?" She reached for the platter of pancakes and passed it to him. "I always wanted a pet. I was going to name my dog Scruffy and my cat Snowball, but my parents wouldn't allow pets in our house."

"Debbie was allergic to animals." He helped himself to a pile of pancakes and then some fried potatoes. Damn, his mouth was watering. "I guess that doesn't matter anymore, does it?"

"So, you were married to Debbie Dalton. I just read

an article about her in *People*. They're calling her a rising star."

He reached for the maple syrup she'd put in a small glass pitcher. It was warm.

"That's nice," he said. "They certainly wouldn't call her mother of the year."

She looked at the mountains in the distance. He dreaded the inevitable questions. She wasn't going to let him eat, and he knew it.

"C'mon, Buck. Tell me what happened. Whatever it was, Caitlin got so traumatized by it, she stopped talking."

He'd just wanted to get a taste of the beautiful pancakes with the warm maple syrup before the questions hit, but suddenly everything looked like wax. He tossed his fork down. He might as well tell her everything. Merry's magic seemed to be reaching Cait, and maybe if she knew a little more…

He took a sip of coffee, sat back in his chair and stretched out his legs. "We'd been married for six years when Debbie decided that she'd had enough. That was just after she'd met some guy in a bar in town, who heard her sing. He was some kind of agent. They went to Vegas, where she divorced me, and eventually they went to Nashville to cut a demo. They stayed three months or so, meeting with the record producers and doing whatever."

"Where were you all this time when she was with him?" she asked.

"Here. Working the ranch."

"And taking care of Cait?"

"She was in nursery school at the time, so I was able

to get the majority of my chores done before she came home. I tried to spend a lot of time with her at night because she was so withdrawn and just pined for her mother, but Cait wouldn't talk to me."

He paused, trying to find the right words.

"Please, go on, Buck."

"I knew from the beginning that Debbie had a dream of becoming a singer, a star. I thought that eventually she'd be happy being here with me and Cait, but she never was."

Merry nodded. It was as if she understood Debbie's mind. Why wouldn't she? She had the same dream, and she was living her dream right now.

"Was she a good mother when she was with Cait?"

"Not particularly." Buck shrugged. "There were times where they'd sing together and Cait would sit next to her when she wrote her songs. Cait had a beautiful voice."

Merry nodded. "Just like her mother."

He ignored that. He didn't think that Debbie had a beautiful voice. Not anymore, not when the package it was wrapped in was so selfish and self-centered.

"The day she left, it got ugly between us. We fought in the barn. I was so damn pissed at Debbie. We said hateful things. Debbie told me that she'd had no intention of ever getting pregnant, and called Cait a brat and a mistake."

Buck washed down his bitterness with a long draw of coffee.

"Oh, Buck." Merry wiped the tears from her eyes with one of Cait's hat-shaped napkins.

"Debbie was in such a hurry to leave that she slid on some wet hay and went down in a heap on the barn floor."

"Oh, no. Then what?"

"Nothing really. I helped her up, and she took a swing at me, but I ducked. I wanted to call a doctor for her, but she couldn't wait to leave. She said, 'If you try to stop me, I'm going to tell everyone that you hit me.'"

"Did Cait hear all this?"

Buck shook his head. "Hell, no. She was sleeping. When I saw her the next morning, I had to tell her that her mother was gone. Cait never spoke to anyone again. I can't explain it, but it was as if she folded into herself. She's hated me since. I guess she blamed me and everyone for not convincing Debbie to stay."

With a flick of his wrist, he tossed what was left of his coffee onto the ground and stood.

Now she knew it all, and she was only one of a few who did. "Thanks for the coffee, but I'd better go. I have things to do."

"But you didn't eat a thing."

"Sorry. Maybe later."

The phone started ringing inside, and he tweaked his hat to Merry and hurried inside to answer it. Normally, he'd let it go, but it might be Karen calling from the hospital.

"I wonder if it's Karen," he heard Merry say behind him.

As he answered the phone, Merry entered the kitchen. "It's for you. It's Joanne." He handed it to her.

"Good morning," she said. A deep frown creased her

forehead. "It was just a harmless dinner." She sat down at the kitchen table with a long sigh. "Joanne, I have to go. Karen is getting out of the hospital tomorrow, and I have things to do."

She clicked off the phone, sighed deeply and looked out of the window. Buck tried to keep busy by loading the dishwasher and wiping off the counter, but soon there was nothing left to do.

"Buck, you should know that our picture hit one of the tabloids this morning. It won't be long before they find out everything about you and what your association is with me. I'm sorry."

"So? It's just a picture."

"It's news. Gossip. People like that kind of thing, or at least the media thinks they do. The headline reads something like 'Domestic Goddess Goes Mex with Cowboy' and the article insinuates that we're having a torrid love affair under the hot Arizona sun."

Buck winked. "Well, we are." He succeeded in getting only a faint smile from her.

She avoided his eyes. "Joanne wants to release something. You know, damage control."

He wanted to throw something. "I see," he said instead. "Damage control."

She didn't meet his eyes. "Buck, I don't mean to hurt you, especially after what you told me about Debbie. I like you a lot."

This whole morning was starting out worse than being bit by a rattler.

"I have my business to think about, just like you have your ranch."

"And sometimes I want to get away from the ranch and my responsibilities."

"Me, too. But I can't." She touched his cheek gently with her palm. "I can't seem to resist you, Buck, but it'll never work out between us."

"Just what I've been thinking." He spit out the words, then stepped away.

Merry somehow looked surprised, relieved and hurt all at once. "You were thinking that, too?"

He shrugged. "Of course." *Dammit.* He'd wanted her to say that it didn't matter—that nothing mattered but their obvious feelings for each other. But she didn't say a word to that effect.

Neither had Lisa or Debbie.

"Well, I have things to do," he snapped. "Make up a grocery list for Cookie. I'll round up the boys and they'll do whatever needs doing around here."

"Thank you." She gave a weak smile but still couldn't meet his eyes. "And don't worry. I'll keep an eye on Cait."

Buck hurried out of the house and headed to the barn, thinking that he would have rather been kicked in the gut by a mule than by Meredith Bingham Turner's new cowboy boots.

Buck let Ty direct the men and handle whatever Merry needed done at the house, and he retreated to the barn. It would keep them all busy while he put the finishing touches on a china cabinet he was making. He did his best thinking while he was making furniture, and he had some major thinking to do.

He thought about the big inventory that was stashed

in the far corner of the barn, all ready to be hauled to Jack's gallery. Dammit, it had to pay off.

He needed to get several more pieces finished soon. He was way behind schedule.

Hell, he would have bet his last dollar that she hadn't been thinking of her business empire last night. But he didn't know what to do about the fact that she thought a relationship with him would mean bad publicity for her. He couldn't help that. He was just a cowboy, and she'd have to take him or leave him.

Hell, she'd made her decision: she was going to leave him. He'd known that right from the start.

"All right, cowboy. Just put her out of your mind. She's just Karen's friend. That's all," he mumbled, as he sanded one of the doors of the cabinet by hand. "We had some fun together. No harm done. Right, Bandit?"

The horse whinnied. If nothing else, at least a cowboy could count on his horse.

A couple of hours later, Buck found Ty eating pancakes and potatoes with Merry under the cottonwood tree. Cait was up, dressed and eating, too. She looked tired, though, and her eyes still looked a little puffy.

He walked over to Cait, gave her a kiss on the cheek and smoothed down her hair. He licked his lips. "You taste as sweet as maple syrup." She should—it was all over her face.

Even if she still didn't respond, she didn't cringe away from him, and that made him feel good.

"I'm going to take a ride over to Gunderson's ranch," he said to Ty. "I have to check out a horse for Doc Goodwater's grandson."

Ty turned to Merry. "Why don't you take a ride with him?"

"Well…um…" She avoided Buck's eyes.

"Go ahead, Merry. It'd do you good to get away from here for a while and see some of the countryside. Right, brother?" Ty gave Buck a pointed look. "Go look at some horses. Cait can help boss us men around. She has Merry's list and she's tough."

Merry looked up at him, and he could see the resolve in the stiffness of her spine. She was probably still thinking about the phone call from her publicist. He guessed that she'd just remembered that she was the boss, and she'd do whatever she wanted.

And Buck Porter was going to be used to make her point.

"I'll bring the truck around," he finally said, feeling trapped.

Ten minutes later, they were bouncing down the main road of the ranch in Buck's ancient pickup.

They managed to make polite, neutral conversation as if their picture had never appeared in the tabloids, like they'd never made hot passionate love, and like there wasn't a chasm in between them as wide as the Grand Canyon.

Buck pointed to the right. "Gunderson's just over that mesa. It's called Buffalo's Back Mesa."

Merry noticed nothing that looked like a buffalo or its back.

Buck turned into a narrow dirt road in between two

huge saguaros. "Gunderson's a tough old bird who's made a fortune selling bull sperm."

"Don't go there," Merry warned.

Buck chuckled. "He's got several prize bulls that he gambled on, and it paid off. People pay thousands of dollars for a straw of sperm."

"You insisted on going there," Merry joked, feeling good that things were back the way they were between them, at least on the surface. "Will I get to see these sperm donors?"

"Sure. Gunderson loves to show them off."

As soon as Buck pulled in, a tall, thin man with a John Deere baseball cap appeared out of a long brick house and waved.

"Hey, Olan."

"Hey, Buck."

They both got out of the pickup. "I'd like to introduce you to a friend of my sister's. Olan Gunderson, this is—"

"Meredith Bingham Turner." The baseball cap came off his head and he crushed it between his hands. "I'd know you anywhere."

"Nice to meet you, Mr. Gunderson," Merry said.

Gunderson wiped his right hand on his jeans, then held it out to her. They shook.

Buck's eyes twinkled. "Olan, I didn't know you were a fan of Merry's."

"Inez will skin me alive when she finds out that Meredith Bingham Turner was right here on our ranch, and she missed her."

"Where is Inez? Is she all right?" Buck asked.

"She's fine. She's at a meeting about the fund-raiser this Saturday night."

Buck nodded. "Doc Goodwater sent me to check out that horse he wants to buy for his grandson, and Merry wanted to see your bulls."

"Is that right, Miss Turner?"

Merry was caught off guard as Buck grinned. "Um...I'd love to see them, Mr. Gunderson."

They walked over to a long, narrow building with dozens of stalls. Many horses were peeking over the half doors. "These are beautiful horses," she told him.

"Call me Olan."

"And I'm Merry."

Gunderson grinned, and his teeth reminded her of horse teeth, big and yellow. "Al Capone."

"Al Capone?" Buck asked.

"That's the horse Goodwater was looking at."

Gunderson unlatched the door, and led Al out. Buck let out a low whistle. "He's a beauty."

"He sure is." Gunderson thrust the horse's rope into Merry's hand. "I'll be right back. I'm going to get my camera. Buck can take a picture of us so Inez will believe that you were really here, Merry."

"Okay." She took a step back from the big horse and let out some slack in the rope.

Buck shook his head in disbelief. "Even Olan Gunderson knows you."

Merry watched as Buck trailed his hands over most every part of Al. His hands were gentle as they moved down the gray horse's neck and legs.

Mesmerized, she remembered how the same hands

moved up and down her body and did such magnificent things.

Even now, just thinking of their lovemaking made her knees buckle. She couldn't manage to look away from Buck, his every move accentuating his taut, muscular body.

Great heaven above, she *had* to stop thinking of Buck. She had already told herself a hundred times that a relationship with him wasn't realistic. She had a job to do here, and she needed to concentrate on it. The last thing she needed was a romance with an Arizona cowboy.

Buck stood and his turquoise eyes scanned the area until his gaze settled on her. He grinned and winked. A tingle started in her stomach and radiated to all her nerve endings, making her whole body hum in excitement.

Merry smiled back and felt all her resolve melting in the afternoon sun—along with her heart.

Chapter Twelve

"Buck, get close to Merry," Gunderson said, camera poised. "And say cheese," he shouted.

"Are you sure you want a picture taken with me again?" Buck whispered to her. "What will your public think?"

Her heart sank. They'd been doing so well, keeping things light. "I can see the headlines now: Domestic Goddess and Cowboy Visit Sperm Bank."

Buck laughed. "Good one."

Buck's arms went around her waist, and her breath caught from his touch.

Olan took the picture—five of them, actually. "Buck, you go ahead and test-drive Al, and I'll take Merry to see the boys."

He slipped the camera into his pocket, took her arm and pulled her away from Buck. They walked through a variety of cacti and some tiny wildflowers. Partridges hurried away in front of them and birds chirped in protest and flew away. Merry thought about how pretty it was, and then she thought about snakes. That was a first for her—she used to think about the snakes first and then notice the scenery after.

"There they are." Olan pointed behind a fence made of thick rusty pipe. "The black one's called Rocket Science. He's a Brahmin. The muley, that's the one without horns, looks like a skunk, doesn't he? His real name is Skunk on Steroids, or Skunky for short. And there's Phantom of the Opera."

Merry saw a cream-colored bull amble toward them.

"Ain't he a beauty?"

Actually, they were all the ugliest things she had ever seen on four legs. Two of them had huge lumps on their backs that swayed as they walked, and they had an assortment of lethal-looking horns, except Skunky. And the huge creatures were all walking toward them now. "Um, Olan...this fence will keep them in, won't it?"

"You have nothing to worry about. It's one-hundred-percent Bethlehem Steel, made in Pennsylvania. In the U. S. of A."

"Good."

The bulls were about five feet away from the fence and they stopped there. She looked into their big black eyes, and respected them immediately. Who was she to argue with a zillion pounds of beef?

She could hear the scrape of boots on the gravel. She turned to see Buck approach.

"Aren't they beauties?" Buck asked.

"Exactly what I was just thinking," Merry lied.

"Cowboys ride bulls like these for sport—and money and buckles."

"Money, I could see…maybe. But buckles?" She shook her head.

He turned to Gunderson, took his hat off and held it to his heart. "Forgive her. She's from Boston," he joked.

Olan chuckled. "Miss Merry, around these parts, a cowboy's belt is like his trophy case."

She laughed, pointing at Buck's buckle, as big as one of his mother's silver platters. "I've noticed."

Buck shook Gunderson's hand. "I'll tell Doc Goodwater that Al Capone is a perfect horse for his grandson. I'd like him myself."

Gunderson nodded at Buck, then pointed at Skunk on Steroids. "You still interested in Skunky?"

"I've always been interested in Skunky, Olan. You know that."

"Just make me an offer. I'd love to sell him to you."

Buck took a deep breath. "Maybe sometime."

A horn beeped and a huge black pickup sped down the drive trailing dust behind it.

Olan turned. "Why, it's Russ Pardee. I wonder what the hell he wants."

Merry saw Buck's hands tighten into fists.

They all watched as the big man lumbered toward them. Russ Pardee was as tall as Buck, but twice as wide and not at all physically fit. His face was red and he was sweating profusely after the short walk.

"Howdy, Olan." Pardee nodded to him, then turned to Buck. "Porter."

"Pardee," Buck mumbled in greeting.

Pardee tweaked the brim of his hat to Merry. "Ma'am."

That was the end of the man's politeness. He turned back to Buck. "So, Porter, have you decided to accept my latest offer?"

"I'm not going to sell my land to you, Pardee. Not while there's a breath left in me."

He grunted. "Someday you will."

"Don't wager all your chips on that," Buck drawled.

"I only bet on a sure thing—like you going under." Pardee chuckled, then turned to Olan. "So, you going to sell Skunky to me?"

Merry noticed that Buck's knuckles were turning white. If there was going to be a fight, she just might be throwing the first punch—at Russ Pardee.

How dare Pardee treat Buck as if he was nothing and turn his back to him?

Her stomach sank. Wasn't that what she'd done this morning?

"I don't have any plans on selling Skunky, Russ," Olan said, turning away from Pardee and winking at her. "I can't part with him, but the others are for sale for the right price."

"I want Skunky," Pardee hissed.

"You must have jalapeños in your ears, Pardee. Olan said he's not for sale," Buck said slowly through gritted teeth. "Neither is the Rattlesnake Ranch. Now, get that through your thick head."

Merry touched Buck's arm. "Buck, I think we'd better get back. I promised to cook a meal for the boys, remember?"

His eyes told her that he wanted to stay and fight, but he eventually nodded.

Buck shook hands with Olan, ignored Pardee, then took her hand and led her to his pickup.

As she settled in the seat, she thought of how Buck wanted to buy Skunky. Obviously, the bull was a good one if Pardee wanted him, too.

Olan wouldn't sell the beast to Pardee. He wanted Buck to have him. That told her that Olan respected Buck enough to wait until he had the money.

But Buck would never have the money.

Merry would like nothing better than to write a check to Olan right now for the animal so Buck could have it. Money didn't mean anything to her, and it meant so much to him.

But he was extremely proud, and she remembered how he flat out told her that he wouldn't take her money.

And she had humiliated him enough for one day.

"I'll bet that you wanted to throw your hat back there," Merry said as they drove away from Gunderson's.

"You'd win the bet. I've been wanting to do a lot of hat-throwing lately."

"Look, I know that what I'm about to say is going to make you mad, but I'm going to say it, anyway. Let me give you the money."

"I'm not going to borrow money from you."

"I'm giving it to you."

Buck snorted just like one of Gunderson's bulls. "No."

"Look, I'm not clueless. I know you have your pride, but it's something that I want to do."

"Donate your money to a worthy cause."

"That's what I'm trying to do."

"No."

"How about if we become partners? I'll front the money, and you can run the business. I have several ventures like that...." She stopped at that. She sounded like she was a major snob, but she didn't mean to be. She was trying to make him understand. "A rodeo-stock contracting business would be another investment for me."

"Or a write-off," he snapped. "Thanks, anyway. I appreciate the offer, but forget it. I have a couple of ideas on the fire."

"You said that before. Care to share?"

"I have something cooking with a friend in Scottsdale. If that plan doesn't work, there's a developer who wants to buy a parcel along the river for condos and a golf course. It'd clear up all of what I owe the bank and then some."

Merry's heart sank. "Oh, Buck, no. Don't do that."

"Maybe I won't have to if Scottsdale works out."

"What do you have going on in Scottsdale?"

"It's not important. Just something that might work, maybe not."

She rolled her eyes. Getting information from him

was like trying to remove cookies from a baking pan that wasn't lined with parchment paper. "I couldn't help overhearing about your bill at the feed store."

"I've got another idea for that."

"Want to share that one?"

"Nope."

Merry let out a sigh of frustration. "What about Skunky?"

"I'm counting on my share of the dude-ranch profits, if there are any, to purchase rodeo stock. Skunky will be my first purchase. Olan will wait."

"Don't sell the land by the river, Buck. Please let me give you the money."

He didn't answer.

Frustrated, Merry blew out a breath. "You're going to lose the best part of the ranch because of your damn pride."

"If it means selling some of it to keep the rest of the place, it'd be worth it."

"What about the water? Isn't that a big thing in Arizona?"

He took a deep breath. "I'd keep the rights. They just want it to make the ninth fairway look pretty and to stick a bridge over it to the tenth hole."

"I can see you have it all figured out. Well, if you won't let me help you, I figure that you'll need the dude ranch even more than ever for your stock-contracting business."

There was more silence. Dead silence.

"Okay, then. When I feature the ranch on my TV show, I guarantee you that you'll have to turn guests away. It'll be a fabulous success. Just what you wanted." Merry took her notebook from her purse and starting writing. She snuck a peek over at Buck and saw a vein bulging in his neck. He wanted his home turned into a dude ranch about as much as he wanted tickets to a Debbie Dalton concert.

"I think we ought to get a menu finalized for your guests," she pressed. "I'll prepare a draft and discuss it with Karen and maybe Cookie. Do you think he can handle doing all the cooking?" She scribbled on the paper. "If not, I should interview for another cook, maybe two. I think we should turn the bunkhouse into a rustic dining hall. It'll probably attract a local crowd, too." She kept writing things down, and watching his vein pump faster. "With a little signage on the main highway and roads, we'd have a good turnout for meals. And don't forget the trail rides and chuck-wagon picnics. We can advertise them in the papers and offer discounts for large groups. We're going to need to train your ranch hands in first aid, the proper way to serve and take away dishes, and other hospitality etiquette. I can work up a short training program."

Buck flicked on the truck's radio and someone singing in Spanish filled the cab of the truck. She got Buck's message loud and clear: he didn't want to hear any talk about the dude ranch or hear any more about her money or his lack of it.

What was she to do then? The stubborn cowboy didn't want her financial help. There weren't any other alternatives.

Maybe she could get Karen to convince him to take her money.

"I'll use the commercial on my next first-run show that airs in three weeks. After that, the Rattlesnake Dude Ranch will be known throughout the United States and Canada."

She flipped the page in her notebook and made more notes. If he only knew that she was jotting down names for her Christmas list instead. She wanted to push him, wanted him to really know what he'd be in for. Maybe then he'd accept her offer of financial assistance.

Finally, they arrived back at the house, and Merry opened the door of the pickup. "Thanks for taking me along to Gundersons."

"No problem."

She half expected him to say more, but he was quieter than usual and he avoided her eyes. Something was still on his mind, and she knew exactly what it was.

She took a deep breath and plunged right in. "Buck, I'm sorry if I hurt you today. It was bad timing on my part, and then I went and offered you money."

He looked up at Lizard Rock, as if he was asking for guidance from his dad and grandfather. "I understand. You have a reputation to maintain. I can't help your career. But I can't take your money, either. That's just the way it is."

She stared at Lizard Rock, too, hoping to sort out what was happening in her own mind. Maybe his ancestors would help him find his way and help her while they were at it.

"Let's forget it. And if it makes you feel better, I'll watch out for cameras when we're out in public together." He smiled, but the twinkle wasn't in his eyes.

She sighed. "Will you be joining us for supper?"

"Wouldn't miss it."

"I'll ring the triangle thing when it's ready."

He nodded.

"Will we be going to the hospital to visit Karen tonight?" she asked.

"Ty said that he was going to visit her and take Cait, so Karen will have company tonight. Besides, she'll be home tomorrow. You can get some sleep tonight since..." He pushed his hat back with a thumb. "Well, since neither of us got much sleep last night."

"That sounds good," she admitted. It would sound even better if she knew that Buck would join her in the tree bed.

Buck couldn't help but admire how Merry could cook up a storm for eight hungry cowboys without seeming overwhelmed. True, she had very appreciative dinner guests, with Cookie leading her fan club, but no one appreciated her genius more than Buck did.

Since she had arrived, he couldn't wait for meals. He loved how she came down to the corral and brought him coffee in the morning. He loved having breakfast under the cottonwood tree. He'd never admit it, but he even liked her turkey chili and had been microwaving the leftovers for a midnight snack.

But most of all, he loved watching her cook. That was why he sat down at the kitchen table with five days worth of junk mail, bills, magazines and a stack of credit card offers. He looked at everything as if each one was the most important piece of literature in this century, but that was just camouflage.

He was really watching her.

Merry hummed as she whirled around the kitchen, chopping this, cutting up that. Her shoes were off, and if he were the type to wax poetic, he would say that it almost looked as if she was doing a ballet or something right in the kitchen.

He continued to secretly watch her, loving every minute, but hated the fact that she'd be leaving in another week.

The ringing of the phone interrupted his thoughts. He began to get up, but she waved him back down. "I can get it."

It was for her—Joanne again. He tried not to listen to her conversation, but what could he do? He was sitting right there.

"Really? My own daily talk show on public TV?"

He got up to get a drink of water, so he could hear better.

"New York City?" Her shoulders slumped, and she pushed back her bangs. "Yes, of course. Yes, it's a wonderful opportunity, and the money is certainly outstanding. I guess I can sublet my apartment in Boston or something."

Buck watched as she became more animated. He half expected her to whip out the notebook she always carried and start scribbling.

He wasn't disappointed. The notebook soon appeared.

"When do I have to be in New York? *Three days?* Oh. I don't know. I have commitments here, but I should be able to wrap things up in three days. Perfect. Wait until my parents hear this."

When she hung up the phone, her eyes sparkled and her cheeks were flushed. "Oh, Buck. Did you hear? My own talk show."

He tried to be as happy for her as she obviously was, but he didn't want her to go. She was good for Cait, good for him. When she'd first arrived, he couldn't wait to get rid of her. Now he wanted her to stay.

He was driving himself crazy.

"That's terrific. Congratulations," he managed to say. He really was happy for her.

Merry did a twirl in the middle of the kitchen. "I have to be in New York in three days."

"I heard."

"I can't wait to call my parents and tell them the good news."

"Go right ahead. Call them," he said, looking over at the chicken frying on the stove. "I can handle things here."

Merry took her apron off. "Turn around."

He did and her arms wrapped around him as she tied the apron around his waist. His heart raced at the contact with her, and fell at the same time. She was leaving. It was too soon. Just too damn soon.

But he already knew that nothing would come of it even if they had all the time in the world. It boiled down to the fact that he was rooted to the ranch, and Merry was rooted to her business.

He always knew it would never work between them.

But that didn't mean that they couldn't enjoy the time they had left. He wanted to make love to her again. Maybe if he did, he could get her out of his system.

Or maybe he just needed a night on the town to get Meredith Bingham Turner out of his mind. He should do a little dancing, toss down a few longnecks and spend the night with a warm and willing woman.

Interesting. Once that would have appealed to him. Now it didn't.

Swearing under his breath about how Meredith Bingham Turner had turned his life into horse droppings in just a few days, he tossed the chicken pieces around in the oil and stirred the potatoes she had boiling.

"Mother, guess what?" he heard her say. She sounded more like a teenager than a successful businesswoman. He smiled as he dragged chicken pieces through some kind of batter. Her parents' approval meant a lot to her.

"I've been offered a daily talk show on public TV," she said. "We tape in New York City, and I'll be interviewing people like designers and craftsmen. And various celebrity chefs will cook with me."

He brought a chair over to the phone and motioned for her to sit. She smiled gratefully. Then he noticed the smile melt right off her face.

"No, Mother. It's not a major network. It's public TV, but it's *daily*." She slumped in the chair and closed her eyes. "Public TV is nothing to sneeze at, Mother. I think it's wonderful."

Obviously, her mother didn't.

Merry shook her head, pushed her bangs back and sighed. "I'm sorry. I have to go now, Mother. I'm cooking for some cowboys." She stood up. "Because I want to cook for them." Her voice cracked. "Give my best to Dad."

She couldn't hang up the phone fast enough. But instead of returning to the kitchen, she headed out the back door. Buck was just about to tell her that the spuds looked done, but he knew she couldn't have cared less.

After listening to Merry's conversation and hearing the pain in her voice, he wanted to help her somehow.

He remembered her conversation with her mother in the hospital—this was the same kind of torture for her. He'd like to tell her that she was never going to please her parents, no matter how hard she tried, so quit trying.

Now he understood a lot more about what made Meredith Something Turner tick. She was a smart woman. Couldn't she see what they were doing to her?

He looked around for pot holders to take the corn bread out of the oven. Where were they?

Merry returned to the kitchen. Her eyes were a bit red. "I can take over from here, Buck."

"Why don't you go take a long bath or lie down for a while? I can finish up in here."

"I do my best thinking while I'm cooking, and my best cooking while I'm thinking," she said.

"Okay. It's all yours. I'll leave you alone."

"No, don't go. Please stay." She looked surprised at her own words. "That is, if you don't have anything important to do right now."

"No. I don't."

He pulled a beer out of the refrigerator, yanked the cap off on the bottle opener on the doorjamb, and took a long draw. "If you want to talk, I'm all ears."

She drained the spuds and began mashing them as if her life depended on it. "It's the same old story. I can never do anything to please my mother. My father will feel the same way. It's not network TV. It's only public TV. As if I'm not good enough. No matter what I do, I'm not good enough."

She flipped a chunk of butter into the pot, poured in some milk and went back to mashing. "I was going to do potato salad, but there wasn't enough time. I hope the boys don't mind mashed."

"They won't mind a bit. And they'll be fighting over your corn bread."

"I love to cook for real people. Now I'm so busy I never get to see people actually sit down and enjoy a meal that I made." She shrugged as she floured some more chicken pieces. "I know the cowboys will appreciate it."

"They sure do, and no one appreciates it more than Cait and I. But your parents don't appreciate you, do they?"

"They never did. And no matter what I do, I can't win."

"Why do you keep trying? Just please yourself."

A piece of chicken hung from the fork she was holding, and Buck could see her hand shake. "I've given up many times, believe me. They've never loved me. Never said they are proud of me. Yet I keep trying to please them. Wanting to hear one word of praise from them."

Buck scooped her into his arms. She lay her head on his shoulder.

"Are you happy with the public TV show?" he asked.

She hesitated. "Yes. I think it'll be fun."

"As long as you're happy, what do you care if anyone else is happy or not? You're all grown up now, in case you haven't noticed. You're on your own, making your own living. You're a success in every sense of the word, Merry. You don't have any ties. You're not…"

"Leaving behind a young daughter?"

"Yeah, that's right. And as long as you're happy, that's all that matters. If your parents can't be happy for you, if it isn't enough for them, then that's their problem."

She smiled and her back straightened. "You're right, of course. I've told myself the same thing a million times."

"Maybe someday you'll believe it."

She stepped away but held on to his hands.

"Work at it," he said. "Say 'I'm happy with my show on public TV, and I don't care about anyone else.'"

She repeated it, but her delivery needed some help.

"Now say it louder and with more enthusiasm."

She did, and it was louder and she was smiling as she said it.

"One more time, Merry, and give it all you've got."

This time when she said it, her voice changed. It was stronger and more confident, and she held on to his hands as if she were drowning and he was rescuing her.

She looked up at him, and something came over her. Buck could see it in her eyes. Her hands went limp in his, and he let her go. Maybe he'd pushed her too far.

He took a deep breath as Merry's hands traveled up his chest. She pulled his head down and kissed him. It was light at first, tentative, but then deepened. She was telling him something, giving him something back, and he understood.

"Thanks, Buck."

He was glad that he could help, but he didn't want her gratitude. He wanted her love. He wanted her in his kitchen, in his bed, in his life. He wanted her to be the mother of his daughter.

Fat chance. She was leaving for New York in three days.

He pressed his lips to hers and lifted her in the air. She clung to him and parted her lips. His tongue met with hers and her moan excited him. Her breasts pressed against his chest and he could smell her perfume. He wanted to carry her into the tree bed and make love to her again. He wanted to explore every inch of her body with his mouth, then start all over. He wanted to...

"Well, well...what have we here?" It was a woman's amused voice.

"Louise?" Buck said, jumping away from Merry as if his lips had been scalded. "What the hell are you doing here?"

"I should ask you two the same question." She dropped the suitcase she was carrying and crossed her arms. Her blue eyes, a little paler than Buck's, twinkled in amusement.

Merry smoothed her blouse and held out her hand. "Hello. I'm Meredith—"

"Meredith Bingham Turner," Louise finished, and shook her hand. "I thought you had more taste than to lock lips with my brother." She shook her head.

Louise looked from Buck to Merry, then back again. She shook her head. "My brother, the lone cowboy, with Meredith Bingham Turner? Actually, I thought you two would have killed each other by now. At least that's what Karen was thinking." She grinned. "Anyone need a good lawyer?"

Buck scooped up Louise and twirled her in a circle. "You passed your bar exam?"

"I think so, but I won't know for sure for a while." Louise sniffed the air. "I sure am hungry, and those cowboys out there are about to start a riot if they aren't fed soon. Can I help shuttle the food outside?"

"Lou, go outside and calm them down." Buck winked at Merry, and held his hand out. "I have some unfinished business that needs finishing."

Merry took his hand and stepped into his arms. When his lips descended on hers, he knew that he'd miss her. How had he ever gotten along without her before?

Three days.

That was all the time he had left with this incredible woman.

Chapter Thirteen

Buck was in the mudroom putting on his boots when Merry walked into the kitchen.

"There you are, Cait," Merry said.

Buck saw Merry pull out a chair at the kitchen table next to his daughter. Cait was eating a peanut butter and jelly sandwich that he'd just made her. Merry took the stuffed cat, which was already occupying the chair, and gently placed it on the table in front of them and sat down.

"Cait, would you like me to fix your kitty's tail? I can sew it up, and Princess will be good as new."

From the darkness of the mudroom, he could see Cait's backbone become rigid. That'd be the day Cait let anyone touch her prized possession.

"I had to fix Bonita's tail a few times, but she didn't mind. I can tell you love your kitty, just like I love Bonita."

Cait got up from her chair, and Buck figured that the discussion was over. As he continued to watch, he had to stop himself from letting out a "yee-haw" when Cait went to a bottom cabinet in the cupboard and handed his mother's old sewing box to Merry.

"Thank you." Merry casually opened the box. "I want to pick out the perfect thread for Princess. There it is. What do you think? Does it match?"

"Yes," Cait said.

Buck felt a chill as his daughter spoke for the first time since he could remember.

She could see Merry's eyes open wide, but she remained calm.

Merry pulled off a length of thread, cut it with a little pair of scissors and tied it in a knot. "Okay, Princess, you're going to be as good as new, just like Aunt Karen. Right, Cait?"

Cait nodded. He watched his daughter as Merry stitched the stuffed animal. Cait didn't take her eyes off her.

"I love it here on the ranch, Cait. I'm going to miss it. You're a lucky girl to be able to see the mountains all the time. You have beautiful horses in your front yard and sunshine all the time and beautiful flowers. And you live in a fabulously grand house with paintings that your grandmother made. And Cait, you have a father who loves you very much." Merry stopped sewing. "You know that, don't you?"

Cait didn't say anything.

Merry kept sewing and kept talking. "Your sandwich looks good. Did your daddy make that for you? Go ahead and eat."

Cait took a nibble out of her sandwich and a swig of milk.

"There. Princess is done. Doesn't she look beautiful?" Merry held it up to Cait, who inspected it and nodded. Merry sat it on the table.

Cait stood. "Will you sew her eye on, too?"

"Sure."

"Wait here."

Merry covered her mouth so as not to shout. Buck did the same thing in the mudroom. He wiped his eyes on the sleeve of his shirt. Merry wiped hers on a napkin hat.

Cait came back into the room and handed Merry what Buck assumed to be the cat's eye. Merry threaded another needle.

"Cait, I'm only going to be here for three more days. I'm leaving on Monday."

Buck heard Merry sniff.

"I'm going to miss you very, very much, sweetie." She sniffed again. "Oh, I didn't want to cry."

Cait passed her another napkin hat, and Merry dabbed at her eyes. "Thank you, honey."

Suddenly Cait's arms went around Merry's neck, and she began to sob quietly.

Merry lifted her up and set her on her lap. "Okay, we can cry together. There's nothing wrong with crying. It makes you feel good. Doesn't it? That's how everyone lets out their pain so it isn't inside them anymore like a big knot."

She rocked Cait. "You can always come and visit me with Aunt Karen. You can take a big plane and you can see all the big tall buildings. We can go shopping and see *The Lion King* at the theater, and you can be on my TV show. Would you like that?"

Cait stopped sobbing but still kept hugging Merry.

"I knew you'd like that. Maybe your father would come, too."

Buck held his breath, sure that Cait would walk away. Instead she nodded.

"I'm going to miss your dad, too. I like him a whole lot."

"Are you going to marry him?" Cait asked.

If Merry was surprised, she didn't let on.

Merry kissed Cait's forehead. "He hasn't asked me to marry him, sweetie."

Cait didn't say anything.

"How about if we make some popcorn and watch the Ariel movie together?" Merry asked.

Cait nodded and went over to one of the cabinets and pulled out a box of microwave popcorn. She took out a pack, unwrapped it, put it in the microwave and punched in some buttons.

Merry laughed. "Looks like you've done this before, Cait."

The girl looked up and smiled. When the snack was ready, Cait deftly used a pair of tongs to remove the hot bag from the microwave, and together she and Merry left to watch their movie.

Buck wanted nothing more than to hear his daughter's sweet voice again, but he didn't want to push her and send her withdrawing back to her shell. So, he finished putting his boots on and went out to the barn.

On his walk over, he realized that he owed Merry a debt of gratitude that he could never repay.

Merry had just gotten back to her bedroom and shut the light off, when she heard a knock on the door.

"Come in." She was hoping that Buck would come to her and she wasn't disappointed.

The door opened, he entered, and he immediately shut the door behind him.

Merry sat up in bed and waited for him to speak.

"Cait spoke to you?" He walked over to the bed and sat down on the edge. "Do you know how long I've waited to hear her voice? How can I ever thank you?"

"I couldn't wait to tell you! But how—"

"I was in the mudroom putting on my boots. I didn't want to disturb the two of you."

"I just love her to pieces. And, Buck, she knows you love her, too."

"Thank you. But her mother doesn't love her," Buck said bitterly. "And Cait is desperate for her mother's love. Debbie doesn't even phone unless I call her assistant and tell her to put Debbie on the line. She doesn't send her any Christmas or birthday presents, either. I buy them."

"Oh, Buck. I didn't know that."

"No one knows."

"What about Princess, that stuffed cat she loves?"

"Her fourth Christmas. I bought it and put 'Love, Mommy' on the card." He took a deep breath. "That's why she never lets go of it."

Tears pooled in Merry's eyes. Her heart ached for Buck and Cait.

"I can't stand to see Cait hurt anymore by that woman. You at least said goodbye to her and prepared her for when you left."

"Of course. I remember how it was when I was young. My parents went on business trips, and even when they were home, they were out all hours of the day and night. I'm not saying that my situation was worse than Cait's. She has aunts and an uncle and a father who care for her, but I know what it's like to feel like an inconvenience, a mistake."

"I never—"

"Weren't you devastated when Debbie left? Think of how a little girl would feel," Merry said. "Her mother walked out on her."

"And so did her father, for a long time. Until I snapped out of it and figured out that I was better off without Debbie."

"Cait hasn't figured that out yet. Someday she will. Until then, just love her."

"I do." Buck played with her fingers. "And maybe someday you'll figure that you're better off without your parents' approval, won't you, Merry?"

"Someday." Her heart pounded against her chest. "And maybe someday, you'll let me give you the money that you need, no strings attached."

"Someday." He kissed her hand. "But until then, come here."

Buck didn't know when he'd be able to be alone with Merry again, but he planned on coming to her room each night until she turned him away or left for New York.

He was so impatient to feel her naked skin against his hands, his body, that he had to stop himself from ripping the thin nightgown right off her. Before he slid out of his pants, he tossed a handful of condoms on the nightstand. He didn't want any interruptions tonight while he fished around for them in his wallet.

When he was around Merry, he was as randy as a high school freshman.

He was already hard just watching her face, dreamy with pleasure. He sucked her nipples into his mouth, and when he laved them with his tongue, her legs fell to the sides, allowing him access. He found her little nub with his thumb, and stroked as her head rolled back in pleasure.

"Buck." She reached for him, and gave a slight gasp, no doubt surprised that he was already rock hard. He hurried to open the condom.

"Damn," he said.

She took it from him and proceeded to unroll it down his hard length. If she didn't calm her hands, it was going to be over too fast.

"Ride me, Merry," he was able to mumble.

She smiled and swung a leg over him. Gripping him at the base, she took him slowly into her. She threw her head back, which made her breasts thrust out perfectly into his hands. He thumbed her nipples, and she started moving, sliding up and down until he thought he'd go crazy. She felt so damn tight, so hot. He held himself in check, gritting his teeth.

"Stop," he ordered.

She bent over to kiss him, her tongue meeting his. In one quick movement, he pinned her under him to finish what she'd started.

She met him stroke for stroke, her legs around his waist until he felt her release, then he joined her.

But he still wasn't satisfied. He wanted her again. He'd never stop wanting her.

Merry awoke to a horn beeping outside. Looking at the sun streaming through the windows and feeling how hot the room was, Merry realized that she had overslept. Checking the clock, she discovered it was eleven o'clock.

She hadn't slept this late since college.

Throwing on her bathrobe, she ran a brush through her hair and hurried out to the living room in time to see Karen, Cait, Buck, Ty and Louise walk in.

"Welcome home," Merry said, giving Karen a hug. "I'm sorry I didn't come to pick you up, but I just woke up. I don't know what happened."

"Didn't you sleep last night?" Buck said, throwing her a wink as he helped Karen sit down on the couch.

He knew damn well she hadn't slept.

Karen patted the cushion next to her, and Merry sat down. "I heard that you have to leave on Monday, so it's time for you to enjoy what little vacation you have left. Buck has told me everything you've been doing. Louise and I can finish the rest with your notes. I know you take good notes. Time for you to have some fun."

"I agree," Louise said.

"Me, too," Ty added. "And I certainly can help out in the fun department. Anyone up for the fund-raiser at the church tonight?"

"I'll stay with Karen and Cait," Louise said.

Karen waved her away. "Get lost, Lou. I'm just going to sleep."

"Nope. I'll stay. I have some reading to do," Louise insisted. "Besides, I'm feeling a little jet-lagged."

"Cait can come with us, if she wants to." Buck turned to Merry. "How about it? It's not Boston, but you'll get a taste of good Arizona cooking, and if I remember right, I promised to take you boot-scootin'. No one's better to dance to than the Lizard Rock Cowboys."

It sounded great, even though she couldn't dance. "I'd love to."

"Then it's a date," Buck said.

Merry had to smile at the sly grin on his face. "I think I'll take a quick shower and then, as long as everyone is here, I'll tell you what I have planned for the dude ranch over lunch."

When she joined them, Karen was camped out on the sofa, and everyone else was draped across chairs. Merry thought again how wonderful it would have been to have brothers and sisters. They were all so close, and she could see the great love and respect they had for one another.

Her heart ached. She was going back to an empty life.

All the money and the fame in the world would never fill the void. Like she always had, she'd keep busy by throwing herself into her work so she wouldn't feel lonely.

For a while, Merry pretended that she was part of their family and that Ty, Lou and Karen were her siblings. But, try as she might, she couldn't imagine Buck as her brother. Her lover and her friend, perhaps, but not her brother.

The afternoon flew by. Merry could tell that excitement was building in everyone about her plans for the dude ranch as she ticked off her suggestions—in everyone except Buck.

Merry waved away Louise's and Ty's help, and made a quick exit to the kitchen to make lunch and to let them talk. For Karen, she heated up some chicken broth and warmed up some applesauce. Then she made an antipasto and garlic bread for the others.

She smiled as Caitlin appeared, started setting the table and making napkin hats.

"Thanks, Cait."

"You're welcome."

They all ate and drank buckets of iced tea, and Buck's siblings never ran out of conversation, but Buck was quieter than usual. He tapped his fingers, looked out the window, and seemed like he was in another world.

Merry pushed everything to the back of her mind until Karen suggested that everyone should get ready for the social. Ty and Buck made a quick exit to the bunkhouse.

"What do you plan on wearing, Merry?" Karen asked.

"I have a new dress and a—"

"No designer dresses in this town," Louise said. "Going to the social means you dig out a clean shirt and a clean pair of jeans and you shine your boots. Although boot-shining is optional."

"Lou, take Merry to my closet and get her a western-looking blouse and a concho belt," Karen said. "And your jeans should fit her perfectly. And, Merry, help yourself to my jewelry. Turquoise would look perfect on you."

"I couldn't."

"Of course you can. It'd be just like our college days when we borrowed each other's things," Karen said.

"Deal," Merry said, giving her friend a hug, wondering why suddenly she was so excited over borrowed western wear.

But she knew the answer. She wanted to look hot for Buck.

Buck let out a long wolf whistle when Merry and Cait appeared on the porch, and it made her feel good. "You ladies look beautiful."

"Why, thank you, Buck," Merry said.

Cait shyly looked up at her father and smiled.

Buck grinned at his daughter, then studied Merry from the tip of her hair to the bottom of her new boots. He even pushed back his hat with his thumb to get a better look.

His smile was sexy. He was sexy. He leaned against his truck with his thumbs hooked through his belt loops and his ankles crossed, as if he had nothing better to do than look at her all night.

And that was fine with her. She was up for an evening out with the handsome brothers.

Louise's jeans were at least a size too small, but Karen and Louise pronounced them perfect. The pastel plaid, long-sleeved blouse and the turquoise jewelry were much more flashy than she was used to, but Karen told her that it made her look younger. Who could argue with that? Her new boots and the silver concho belt were the perfect touches.

Under Buck's approving gaze, she felt beautiful and desired.

Buck opened the door of his pickup and helped Cait buckle up in the small backseat. Then Merry got in.

Ty climbed in after her and immediately put his arm around her shoulder. When Buck flashed him a stormy look, Ty chuckled, and his arm returned quickly to his side.

Hmm…she liked that.

They bumped shoulders all the way to town as Ty teased Buck and Buck teased him back. Merry soon got into the spirit of things and got in some zingers of her own. The mood was light, which was just what she needed.

The social was in the basement of a fairly modern church. Round tables with royal-blue tablecloths were set up around an already crowded dance floor. Long buffet tables by the kitchen sported several large vats of food along with a dozen Crock-Pots in various shapes and sizes.

Merry took a whiff of the air and could smell cumin

and tomatoes and jalapeño peppers. The Lizard Rock Cowboys were off to the right on a raised platform and were yodeling in the middle of a song about ropin' and ridin'. To the right of them was a long dessert table filled with cakes, pies and cookies.

She was itching to sample everything and get some recipes from the ladies. Church socials, county fairs and the like were a gold mine of great recipes. She had been collecting them for years now in preparation for another cookbook about old family favorites.

Ty and Buck stood in front of the check-in table with two elderly ladies who were tittering and giggling together like schoolgirls.

The brothers were arguing over who was going to pay the admission fee. She heard the ladies ask them to buy raffle tickets for either a quilt made by Inez Gunderson or for six quarts of Sarah Taft's prize-winning, prickly pear cactus jelly.

Merry finally figured out that the ladies were in fact Inez and Sarah and they were involved in a friendly competition.

She quickly found her wallet and handed Inez a hundred dollar bill. "These two gentlemen are my guests along with the young lady, and please split the rest equally toward the raffle for that beautiful quilt and the jelly." She turned toward Sarah. "Also, can I have the recipe for the jelly?"

"Why sure, honey," Sarah said, obviously pleased. "Why…why…aren't you Meredith Bingham Turner?" She elbowed her friend. "Inez, you old hen, didn't you recognize Miss Turner?"

"I thought it was Meredith, but I wasn't sure. Olan said you were out to the ranch, but I thought he was pulling my leg." Inez smiled up at Merry. "I love your show. I watch you every Tuesday. I have all your cookbooks. And your cookware."

"Me, too," echoed Sarah. "And I have your shower curtain with the ducks on it, in green and yellow."

"Thanks, ladies," Merry said, offering her hand to shake. But Sarah and Inez wouldn't hear of only a handshake.

They both came from around the table and gave her big bear hugs.

Ty and Buck watched in amusement. But Merry recognized something else in Buck's eyes, and knew immediately that he wasn't happy that she'd paid their way into the social.

He was about to protest, but she shot him a look that said "Get over it."

Inez bellowed over the Lizard Rock Cowboys, "Hey, everyone, Meredith Bingham Turner is here!"

The Cowboys stopped yodeling, the dancers stopped dancing and people set their Crock-Pots and covered dishes down. The crowd started moving toward her like a tidal wave. She grabbed Buck's arm in reaction. Ty moved to her other side and put an arm around her waist.

"Whoa," Buck said, holding out a hand like a traffic cop to stop them. "Meredith is going to be here all night. No sense stampeding her. Besides, she's been working real hard at the Rattlesnake with Karen being sick and all. She needs a little relaxation. That's why we came here tonight. And also because she wanted to support this worthy cause."

She never knew Buck was such a natural public relations person, and she liked him a lot more than Joanne. Too bad she hadn't given a thought to the worthy cause—all she'd thought about was going on a date with Buck.

Buck signaled the Lizard Rock Cowboys, and they launched into a drinking song. Some of the guests returned to dancing, others filed into a line and waited patiently to meet her.

After a while, she told Buck, Cait and Ty to go and have fun, that she was okay. Ty drifted off and she saw him kicking up his heels with a variety of women, but Buck was never more than a few yards away. She noticed that he was keeping watch over her, and that made her feel all warm and tingly inside.

Then she watched as he squatted down before Cait and talked to her. She nodded. Then he lifted her into his arms and danced with her.

The happy expression on the little girl's face as Buck twirled and danced with her made her smile.

Inez must have seen her watching and whispered in her ear, "Caitlin is coming along, isn't she?"

"I think so."

"That's wonderful."

"It really is," Merry added, absentmindedly signing another autograph.

For loving his daughter like he did and dancing with her in his arms, Merry lost her heart to Buck Porter forever.

She thought of how her father had never danced with

her. How he'd never picked her up in his arms or made her giggle. She couldn't understand why not. She'd been as perfect as she could be. She'd kept a tidy room, was a good student and had tried not to bother them too much. But she just wasn't perfect enough.

When the dance was done, Buck gently set Cait down, and she ran off to be with the other kids.

Merry continued to talk to each and every person. When the last fan was gone, Buck was instantly at her side. "Let's get something to eat."

"Sounds good."

As they stood in the food line, Merry asked for recipes and listened attentively to old stories. Finally, Buck steered her and Cait to a quiet table in the back of the room and she was able to sit down and eat. They sat side by side with their shoulders touching, sampling each other's food. She was content, feeling comfortable in Buck's company, but fully aware of every inch of him.

They were left to themselves, probably because when someone started walking toward them, Buck's "get lost" look sent them scurrying away.

Some kids came to take Caitlin away for some organized games. Merry went back to the buffet table for some more enchiladas as Buck headed for the bar. Judging from the expression on Buck's face, he was in serious conversation with Dan from the feed store. Whatever it was, it didn't take long until they shook hands and separated. They both looked miserable.

Merry wondered what that was about, and hoped everything was all right. Keeping an eye on him, she went back to the table and scribbled down a recipe for Cattle Drive Stew in her notebook before she forgot what Mrs. Whitney told her.

"Hey, what's this I hear about you, Bucklin? I heard that you're going to be running a sissy dude ranch."

Merry tensed and saw that the sarcastic falsetto voice belonged to none other than Russ Pardee.

"You hear right, Pardee," Buck answered quietly.

"I'll bet your daddy and your grandpa are turning over in their graves."

Ty appeared at Buck's side. Four burly cowboys got up from their chairs and stood at Pardee's side, making a point of sticking out their chests and tucking in their shirts. Three of the ranch hands from Buck's ranch got up and stood by him and Ty.

Merry took a deep breath along with everyone in the room and quickly walked over to Buck. When he saw her approaching, he motioned for her to stand away. She stood at the end of the dessert table.

Buck's knuckles were white around the beer bottle, but to his credit, he smiled and turned his attention back on Pardee. "I imagine my daddy and my grandfather would say that I should do whatever I need to."

"Because you're going under?" Pardee threw his head back and gave an evil laugh. "I never thought you had a head for business. But my offer still stands. I'll buy you out at any time. Just say the word."

"There ain't a snowball's chance in the desert that I'd ever sell to you." Buck casually took a sip of beer, then put the bottle on the bar. "Now, let's quit this conversation and get back to the party."

"Are you stupid, boy? I said I'd buy you out." Pardee's voice boomed over the crowd as a priest hurried over.

"Mr. Pardee, I think you've had a bit too much to drink," the priest said. "Maybe one of your friends should drive you home."

"That's an excellent idea, Father Dolan," Buck said, walking away.

"Don't turn your back on me, Buck Porter," Pardee yelled, grabbing Buck's arm.

"Let go of me, Pardee. Or let's take this outside," Buck said, his voice low and controlled.

It all happened so fast, Merry couldn't tell who threw the first punch, but she was able to save a beautiful lemon meringue pie just before the dessert table collapsed from Buck's and Pardee's weight.

A dozen men rushed across the dance floor and jerked up Pardee and his henchmen, holding back their arms.

Red-faced, Pardee lunged at Buck, but the men held him back. "I'll be there at the tax auction, Porter, and I'm going to buy your ranch right out from under you."

Chapter Fourteen

Merry hurried to Buck and checked for broken bones to assure herself that he was all right. She'd been worried about him. Pardee outweighed Buck by a good forty pounds, but Buck had held his own.

His shirt was torn, and he had a red mark on his chest. "Are you okay? Do you need a doctor?"

"No, I'm okay." He tried to wink, but flinched in pain.

His eye was puffy, and she gently moved his chin to get a closer look. "You're going to have a black eye."

She didn't know what else to do to help him, so she picked up a stack of napkins that had slid to the floor and eyed his shirt. "Let me get some of this mess off you."

"Forget it. It's hopeless."

He slipped out of his shirt that was covered in

frosting and pudding and whatever, and wadded it into a ball. There were more red marks on his chest and arms. She let out a breath of frustration, hating to see his beautiful body all bruised and battered.

"I'm fine." He took her hands and held them. He smiled. "Thanks for worrying about me, though."

She nodded. "Of course I worried about you. I don't want you hurt."

He looked pleased to hear that. Probably because no one ever worried about Buck. He always seemed so strong and capable.

Inez and Sarah appeared with cleaning supplies and shook their heads as they saw the massive mess on the floor.

"What'll we do for dessert now?" Sarah asked.

"First, someone signal the band to start playing," Merry said, springing into action. "And let's get a crew together to clean up the mess. I'll need another crew to help me in the kitchen—I have a plan." She turned to Buck. "I think you'd better get cleaned up yourself. It's all over your jeans."

"Come with me," said Father Dolan, leading Buck away.

Inez and Sarah made quick work of drafting volunteers. Ten people joined Meredith in the kitchen.

Merry looked around at the contents of the cupboards and the refrigerator. Then she spotted exactly what she needed: two bushels of apples. "Are those for anything special?"

Inez shook her head. "I brought them back from my trip to Washington State for whoever wanted them."

"Apple crisp," Merry decided. "Let's make that. It'll bake quickly if we put it in shallow pans. We just need a bunch of people to cut and peel apples."

"Count me in," Ty said, then turned to the volunteers around him. "Right?"

"Right," everyone agreed.

"Great. Cait and I will make the topping," Merry said, grabbing sugar, flour and cinnamon from the cupboards. "Right, Cait?"

"Right. I'll help you, Merry."

Ty's jaw dropped when he heard Cait answer, and Merry gave him a wink. He mouthed the words "I love you" to Merry, and she couldn't help but laugh.

"I'll have some vanilla ice cream delivered from my shop," said a man in a red flannel shirt.

Everyone got into the spirit of things and the many pairs of hands made quick work out of the apple crisp. Soon the smell of apples and cinnamon scented the air.

An hour later, the apple crisp was a hit: "especially since it was made by Meredith Bingham Turner and her assistant, Caitlin Porter," Inez said over the band's microphone.

Merry saw Cait grin when the spectators started clapping, and she didn't hide her face. If only Buck were there to see her!

What a night, Merry thought later as she cleaned up the kitchen. The Lizard Rock Cowboys had everyone up for a two-step but the crowd was thinning.

Buck stepped into the kitchen with a cheerful "hello," and Merry couldn't stop laughing as she studied him.

He was fresh from a shower, and he wore a football

jersey of bright Kelly-green with "Lizards" written across his chest in yellow. The shirt didn't quite reach his stomach, so she could see his tight stomach muscles above the waistband. The stretchy pants clung to his muscular thighs.

She couldn't take her eyes off him.

"Courtesy of Father Dolan, and the Lizards' football team."

Her eyes traveled down his hard thighs and she laughed. "Cowboy boots instead of spikes?"

"Pretty bad, huh?" He looked down at his legs, where the football pants ended and his black boot tops began. He laughed, then sobered when he looked at her. "I'm sorry if I spoiled your evening, Merry."

"Spoiled my evening? Absolutely not. I had a great time." And she had. She'd met a lot of wonderful people and collected a lot of great recipes. And she'd never forget how touched she'd been when she watched Buck dance with Cait.

"Ty said you haven't left the kitchen since the fight."

"That's not true. Cait and I helped serve the apple crisp."

"You got Cait to do that?" Buck's heart melted. "Another miracle by Merry."

Through the serving window, he watched as Cait held up a piece of yarn. A small kitten jumped for it as Cait laughed.

"You really saved the day," he continued. "Inez and Sarah will be talking about it for years." He tried to hook his thumbs in his belt loops, but there were none, so he gave up. "But you never even danced."

She dried one of the big pans that they used for the apple crisp and set it down. "Nope. These boots are still scoot-free and the Lizard Rock Cowboys just signed off for the evening."

"We can't have that. I brought you here to dance, so we should dance." He turned on an old blue radio that sat on a shelf over the sink. After some fiddling, George Strait's unmistakable voice came over the radio.

"I really don't know how to two-step, Buck. It wasn't a recognized dance at the Phillips School on Beacon Hill. Let's wait for a waltz."

"Just follow me," he instructed, sliding a hand around her waist, and intertwining his other hand with hers. "Yeow," he said, none too quietly as she stepped on his feet. "Will you relax?"

She chuckled as she stepped on them again. "Oops...sorry."

"Don't worry about it. That's why cowboys wear boots."

"You should get steel-toed ones if you're going to dance with me."

She was getting the hang of the two-step just as George sang his last note, but Buck didn't make a move to let her go. He swayed with her in his arms to a tractor commercial. Gazing up into his eyes, she saw something there. Something she couldn't define.

As if by magic a slow song came on the radio, and he held her tighter. She noticed that Buck was breathing as hard as she was.

Threading her fingers through his hair, she felt him tense, then he bent over and crushed his lips to hers. Her hands moved lightly under the jersey, across his chest. She didn't want to aggravate any injuries he may have. His skin was warm and smooth, and she let her palms rest against his nipples.

Boldly, she kissed him, feeling his power surge under her palms as he kissed her back. His tongue stroked the length of hers and her knees buckled. He pulled her tighter.

"I'm going to miss you," he said.

"I'll miss you, too." She didn't want to talk. She wanted to feel his lips on hers.

"I'm sorry. I don't know what's come over me," he said. Without meeting her eyes, he took a deep breath and adjusted the waistband of the football pants. "It's getting late. I'll get Ty and Cait, and pull the truck around front." He turned to leave.

She was stunned by his sudden departure. Was he having regrets? "Wait, Buck. I'd like to talk to you about something."

He turned back and waited.

"I found out that the kitten Cait is playing with is available for adoption. It belongs to a Mrs. Prestin. She's sitting over there." Merry nodded to the far corner of the hall. "She's counting up the proceeds with Inez Gunderson. She tells me that this is the only kitten that hasn't been adopted from the litter. Let Cait have it. Please, Buck?"

He didn't know why he didn't think of getting her a cat before. "Sure, she can have it, but she has to take care of it."

"She will."

Merry was as excited as if she were getting the cat herself.

"Go tell her. I want to see her reaction."

He took her hand. "Come with me."

"She'll be so excited, Buck." Merry hesitated. "But it should be a private moment between you and Cait."

"And you're the one I want to share it with. Come on."

Buck and Merry sat down on the floor of the hall and watched Cait play with her new kitten.

Buck smoothed his daughter's hair back and rubbed her cheek with a finger. Merry saw that he was blinking back tears.

He picked up the little ball of fluff and handed it to his little girl. Her hands reached out to take it and she buried her face in its gray fur. She kissed it between the ears and looked up at him, then at Merry.

"I hope you enjoy your new kitten, sweetie," Buck said.

"Thank you, Daddy."

As he looked at his daughter's happy face, Buck squeezed Merry's hand.

Then he whispered in Merry's ear, "My little girl called me Daddy. I've waited two years to hear that again."

Merry squeezed his hand and wished she were able to give him a kiss.

Buck looked through the stack of saguaro ribs he had in a wooden barrel in the corner of the barn. He needed a certain circumference to match the ones he'd lined up for the door of the cabinet he was working on.

It was one o'clock in the morning, and he knew he'd

never be able to sleep—not with Meredith Bingham Turner on his mind.

The door squeaked open and automatically his eyes sought out the holster that he had hooked over a corner of Bandit's stall, but he relaxed when out of the corner of an eye he saw Merry walk in.

"Buck?"

"Yeah?" He turned to face her. He knew he'd have to tell her what'd been on his mind sooner or later, might as well be sooner.

"You walked out here in the dark? That's pretty brave for a city slicker, considering that a snake crossing runs in front of the house. Didn't you see the sign?"

"Very funny." She lifted her long bathrobe and showed him her boots. "I saw the light on, and I thought you might be here. I wanted to talk to you."

"Go right ahead." He brushed the dust and hay off of a metal chair and motioned for her to sit down. He sat on a bale of hay opposite her. But she didn't sit. Instead she inspected the cabinet he was making.

"This is just exquisite!" She turned and stared at him, her mouth gaping open. "Why...why...you're the one who made all the furniture in the house, aren't you?"

He nodded.

"The tree bed, too?"

"Yes."

"Oh, Buck, I love the tree bed!"

"Thanks. It's my favorite, too." At least it was now, since every time he looked at it, he'd remember how they'd made love in it.

She ran the palm of her hand across the top of the cabinet, and Buck remembered the way her hands had felt on his chest in the kitchen of the church. He took a deep breath, wondering how to tell her everything that was in his heart, wondering if he could ever ask her to stay, wondering if she'd ever be happy on the ranch.

"This is beautiful craftsmanship. You are so talented. You're an artist, just like your mother."

He was proud of his work and proud that she thought of him as an artist. "I just like to putter," he said humbly. "I can look at a pile of wood and see it as a cabinet or a dresser or a bookcase."

"Just like your mother could look at a white canvas and make it come to life."

Damn, she makes me feel good.

She turned to him with a surprised expression on her face. "This is your Scottsdale project, isn't it? You're making furniture to sell at a gallery."

He nodded.

"You have more pieces?"

"A couple dozen or so."

"Can I see them?"

"Sure."

She followed him to the corner of the barn where he had everything stored. He lifted the drop cloths for her as she examined each piece, touching the wood, opening the doors of the cabinets and the drawers.

"Everything is just...so unique. Just beautiful. I want to buy it all." Turning to him, she said, "You'll make a fortune."

"Good. That's my plan."

"Buck, why didn't you tell me? I never thought that you made those pieces in the house. I thought that someone else...Why on earth didn't you tell me?"

He shrugged. "I guess I never thought it was a big deal."

She shook her head. "It is a big deal. It's another side of you that I wish I'd known."

She went over to a white drop cloth draped over his most valued possession. "Is this another masterpiece? Can I take a peek?"

"It's a masterpiece, but it's not what you think."

Puzzled, she hesitated.

"Go ahead," he said.

She gave a yank and there it was, gleaming in the overhead light. He had just finished dusting it off and shining it up.

"The motorcycle your grandfather gave you?"

He nodded. "It's a 1948 Panhead. The first Harley made with a special motor. You see, the motor is... Well, it's not important."

His gut constricted. He wanted her to cover it back up. He couldn't stand looking at it any longer.

"It looks brand-new," Merry said.

"I've kept it mint. And, like I said before, I haven't had time to ride it much. Not lately, anyway." He took the drop cloth and covered the bike back up.

She looked up at him with those big green eyes. "I know what you mean. I don't have time for anything I like to do, either."

"And what would you like to do, Meredith Bingham Turner?"

She sat on the chair, and he sat on the hay. "What's your dream?"

"Hmm…" She stretched and her eyes closed. "I'd like to bake and cook and experiment with new recipes. I don't want to do it as part of my business anymore. Just for myself and for someone who appreciates it. I'd really like to fire Joanne. And I thought about what you said a lot, and I don't want to beat my head against a wall anymore trying to please my parents or the public. And I want to make my new talk show a success."

"Good for you." Buck clapped. "Go for it."

She stood up and took a bow. "Now, what's your dream, Bucklin Floyd Porter?"

"Sometimes I'd like to jump on that Harley and ride off into the sunset for a while. I think that I need a break from the Rattlesnake, sad to say. And then there's the stock contracting, like I told you before. I'd like to have a go at that. And I'd like to hire a good foreman to take care of some of the small stuff on the ranch, so I could spend more time making furniture. I like doing it." He ticked all his wishes off on his fingers. "And if by some chance I won the lottery, I'd buy out Karen and Lou and Ty and let them follow their dreams."

Her eyes were as wide as saucers. "You know that they don't want to stay on at the ranch?" She shook her head. "And they thought that they were keeping everything such a secret."

"Of course I know. I know that Karen wants to start a nursery-and-landscaping business in town. I know that Ty wants to wander a bit and find himself. And I know that Louise wants her own law firm."

Merry smiled. "Boy, your family sure can't keep secrets."

"I know they help out on the ranch because of me."

"You've done a lot for them, Buck. Every one of them."

"But it's because I wanted to. They don't owe me. They don't owe me a thing."

"Have you ever told them that?"

No. He admitted to himself that he never had. "I guess I should. I think they need to follow their own dreams, not mine."

She stood and held out her hands to him. They felt small and delicate in his and he closed his big, calloused hands around hers. He wanted to protect her forever, from the tabloids, from anyone who could hurt her.

"Don't sell the land by the river, Buck. I think your furniture business will be a real success," she said. "I really wish you'd told me about it earlier. We could have done a segment on it."

"I'm a rancher, not a furniture-maker."

"You're both."

"Maybe, but if you think this stuff will sell, I'll wait and see how the sale turns out. Maybe I'll get some orders and I can show the bank that I'm not a lost cause."

"It'll sell all right. Now, what about the dude ranch?"

"Maybe Jack will move my shindig up and we'll take it from there."

"He'll do it." She put her arms around his neck and met his gaze. "You know, Buck, in a way, we've both devoted our lives to others, haven't we?" she said. "Me to pleasing my parents, and you to the legacy of the Rattlesnake Ranch. And don't forget how you've raised your sisters and brother and sent them to college. That's no small accomplishment."

He shrugged. "I guess I never looked at it that way. It was something that I just did."

"Think about it. It's time for you to start living your dream." She hated to leave him, hated to leave Cait and the ranch. "Well, I'd better say good night."

"Merry, wait. There's something I want to tell you." He dropped her hands and paced in front of the stalls, his voice getting louder with each word. "I love you, dammit, but where is that going to get me? You're leaving for your New York job and I'm staying. You'd never be happy here, and I wouldn't be happy in the city. Sounds like a standoff to me."

Her jaw dropped. *"You love me?"*

Hadn't she heard a word he'd said? "Of course I do. I think I fell in love with you the day you arrived. When you were worried that I'd shoot the burros."

"You love me?"

"Yes, I love you! Can't you tell? You've been driving me crazy ever since you came here."

"I've been driving you crazy?"

"Yes."

"You don't know what crazy is." She rubbed her temples. "And you love me. Doesn't that beat all?" She hurried toward him and stood toe to toe in front of him. "You are such a blockhead, Bucklin Floyd Porter." She turned and paced, stirring up dust and hay. "I love you, too." She kicked at a bale of hay.

"Hey, you're the one who didn't want to be seen with me."

"I was a fool about the pictures. That'll never happen again as long as I live." She put her hands on her hips. "Well, what are we going to do?"

"Nothing."

"Nothing?" Merry felt the heat rush to her face. She was so mad, she was ready to explode. "We love each other, and that's that?"

"If we got married, you'd get bored here and you would leave."

"You don't know that."

"I know. You have too big of a career to be happy here for any length of time."

Merry realized where he was coming from. "Buck, I'm not Debbie."

He didn't even react to her comment. "We can visit each other. When you get time off, you can fly here. And when I get time off, you can fly here."

She pulled on her earlobe. "Somehow that didn't come out right, or I didn't hear it right."

"Then there's the other thing."

"What other thing?" she asked.

"The money thing. You have it and I don't. You know that bothers me."

"Here we go again."

"There's no way I'm going to be a kept man."

"You are truly a caveman." Her eyes looked to heaven. "And that's your final word on it?"

"Yes."

Merry stood her ground even though her heart was breaking. "You're absolutely right, Buck. There's no hope for us. I must have lost my mind to think that we could be happy together. And I hoped for a moment that we could work things out, but I guess you don't want to try." She blinked back tears. "Good night."

He reached for her and pulled her to him. She let her cheek rest on his chest, let his hands travel up and down her back. "How about one more day together? Just the two of us?"

She knew she couldn't handle that, so she made an instant decision. "Sorry. I'm going to leave tomorrow afternoon. I have to start making some of my dreams come true. There's nothing for me here."

She was just about to head for the door when Buck gripped her shoulder and turned her around.

"Wait, Merry. I need to… Cait? Honey, what's the matter?"

It was then that Merry saw Cait in her nightgown. She was holding her stuffed cat and standing just inside the barn door. Tears were dripping down her face, and she had the hiccups.

She ran to Merry. Taking Merry's hand, she pulled her toward the door.

Merry dug in her feet. "Cait. Stop. What's the matter?"

"He's going to hit you and push you because you are leaving! Run, Merry! He's going to hit you like he did my mommy."

Merry looked over at Buck. It looked like he was frozen in shock. Suddenly, he seemed to defrost right before her eyes. The color came back into his face.

"Cait, honey…did you think I hurt your mommy?"

"I heard her say she was going to tell that you hit her and pushed her and that I was a mistake. I was a brat."

"You were in the barn that night, Cait? Just like now?"

Tears streamed down her cheeks as she nodded.

Buck knelt down on one knee in front of her. "Cait— I didn't hurt your mommy. She slipped on some wet hay. She was okay. I would never, *never* hurt anyone like that. Please believe me, Caitie. I would never hurt Merry, either. I—I love her."

Her eyes grew wide. She looked at Merry, then to her father, than back again.

"It's true, Cait," Merry said. "Your father is a kind, wonderful person who loves you with his whole heart. He'd never hurt you or me or your mommy. And I love him, too. And you're not a mistake or a brat. You are the sweetest girl I've ever known. I wish you were mine."

Cait swiped her arm across her face to wipe her tears. Then she picked up her stuffed cat from the floor and walked into her father's arms.

In stunned silence, Merry and Buck looked at each other. Buck sat back down on the bale of hay and rocked his child. Merry could see his hands shaking.

She sensed that father and child needed to be left alone, so she slipped out the barn door, went onto the front porch and sat in a chair. Looking up at the stars, she thought about her stay at the ranch, and the two people who had come to mean the world to her.

And wondered what she would do without him.

Merry called the airline when she got back to her room. The earliest flight she could get was at three the next afternoon. That was okay. She'd head out in the morning to allow some time to get lost. Then she'd drop off the rental car and check in early.

But first, she'd have breakfast with Karen, Cait and Louise and say her goodbyes to everyone.

She had already said all she had to say to Buck in the barn.

As she slipped into the tree bed for the last time, it took on a new meaning for her because now she knew that Buck had made it along with all the wonderful furniture in the house.

She reminded herself to tell Karen that they could make a lot of additional money if they'd make it known to the dude-ranch guests that the furniture could be made to order. That is, if Buck was interested, and if they ever did get the dude ranch up and open for business.

Knowing that Buck loved her but wasn't willing to try to make things work made her feel empty and hollow, and a gut-wrenching loneliness settled in her heart.

Finally, she had found a man she loved who came with a family she adored along with a sweet daughter, a home and history, but somehow he didn't care enough to want to find some kind of compromise.

Because he thought he was being noble and letting her leave for her own good?

Sheesh.

Because of her finances?

Ridiculous.

But what would it take to make a stubborn cowboy come to his senses and realize that they could make each other happy?

It was all so impossible.

She kept hoping, waiting for a knock on the door. Kept waiting for him to tell her that he'd been wrong and they could work everything out. Kept waiting for him to come into her room and talk about the incident with Cait.

Merry smiled. It was a big breakthrough for them both. Now Buck finally knew what had shocked Cait into a two-year silence. She'd heard—and misunderstood— the fight between Buck and Debbie. She'd been petri- fied of her father, heard her mother say terrible things about her. On top of everything, Debbie had left them.

Merry fell into a restless sleep. At sunrise, tires crunching on the gravel and men talking outside her window rudely awakened her. Getting up, she looked out and saw Dan from the feed store talking to Buck. They were both standing behind a black truck that towed a large metal trailer.

Buck and Dan disappeared into the barn, but came out minutes later. Buck was walking his motorcycle. He paused when he got to the back end, then both men pushed it up the ramp and into the trailer.

Merry's heart sank as she watched Dan scribble something on a long sheet of paper, then hand it to Buck. Buck gave it only a quick glance, then folded and stuffed the paper into his back pocket.

The fool. He had just paid his debt to Dan with his Harley.

They shook hands and Dan towed the motorcycle away.

Buck watched it until it disappeared from sight, then

he took off his hat, flinging it into the desert with a flick of his wrist.

Her heart ached for him.

Buck had just turned back from retrieving his hat when Ty came galloping from the direction of the bunk-house, waving his arms and shouting something that she couldn't make out. Buck nodded, went into the barn and galloped off on Bandit.

Something was wrong.

Merry hurried to get dressed to see if she could help.

Chapter Fifteen

"Some of the cattle are stuck in a wash. If they don't get them out, they'll starve," Karen explained at breakfast. "It's really nothing to worry about. It happens all the time."

Neither Karen nor Louise said anything about Buck selling his motorcycle to pay off Dan. Merry doubted that they even knew.

Louise handed her the morning paper. "You're going to really love this."

On the front page, Merry saw a full-page, color photo of the brawl at the church social. Buck was sprawled out on the collapsed table surrounded by mangled desserts. She stood nearby grinning like a fool and looked like she was about to toss the lemon meringue pie.

She closed her eyes and mustered the courage to read the headline. With one eye barely open, she read, "Meredith Bingham Turner and Date Buck Porter of Lizard Rock, Arizona, Involved in Brawl at Church Benefit."

In spite of herself, she laughed. With her big grin and Buck draped over a broken table and those headlines, it seemed as if *she* was the one who had put *him* there.

If anyone actually read the article, they would get the full explanation. Actually, the story itself was quite flattering, describing how she'd saved the day with her apple crisp after the dessert table was ruined.

It was only the local Lizard Rock paper. With any luck they didn't participate in the wire service and no other paper would pick it up. If they did, taking into account the difference in time zones, the phone would ring, just…about…now….

And it did.

"I'll get it. It's my mother," Merry said.

Karen and Louise looked at each other, then at her.

"You'll see." She got up and answered the phone. Sure enough… "I was expecting your call, Mother. Read anything in the *Boston Globe* about me?"

At one time she would have died, now she didn't give a hoot. She'd made several business decisions during her time with Buck. For one, she was going to downsize her company.

"Mother, I'm flying back to Boston this morning. Then I'm packing for New York City. When I get home, I'd like to have a long talk with you and Dad."

After Merry hung up, Karen clapped. "About time."

"It is, Karen. It is. I made a lot of decisions here, most of which came from conversations with your brother."

Louise giggled. "I take it you don't mean Ty."

"I mean Buck." It was hard to say his name. It was even harder to keep her tears in check.

Karen put her hand over hers. "You've fallen for him, haven't you?"

Merry sighed. "Hard."

"And how does he feel about you?"

"It's mutual, but he's being noble and pigheaded. It's the age-old rich-TV-cook-and-poor-stubborn-cowboy story." She tried to joke through her tears, but her joke fell flat. "And he thinks I'm like Debbie. And then there's the geographical problem. Nothing's going to blast his jeans from this ranch."

"He can be stubborn, but usually he works through it. You just have to hang in there with him," Louise said. "Please do. I've never seen Buck so happy and miserable at the same time. I just knew he was in love. And you're just what he needs."

"Well, he has the next move." Merry mustered a small smile, and put her coffee mug into the dishwasher. "Well, I'd better pack up and hit the road."

"Can't you give Buck a little more time?" Karen asked.

"He knows where to find me." She smiled hopefully.

"We can't thank you enough for all your help," her friend said, hugging her. "Lou and I can take over from here."

"Let me know when—*and if*—you want to proceed with the dude ranch. I'll hold off on airing the commercial until you give me a call. Speaking of calls, can I use the phone in Buck's office? I need to take care of something."

"Sure. Go ahead," Karen said.

She walked down the hallway to Buck's office. Leaning against the desk, she picked up the phone and dialed the number of the Lizard Rock Feed and Hardware Store, displayed prominently on a desk calendar.

"Hi, this is Meredith Turner. Would you give a message to Dan as soon as he returns?"

Merry stood in front of the ranch house and looked at all the friends she'd made during her stay at the Rattlesnake Ranch who came to see her off. Her gray rental car was loaded. All she had to do was to say her goodbyes and get in.

Cookie held his hat over his heart. The ranch hands tipped their hats and joked about how they dreaded going back to the old man's cooking. Buck handed Bandit's reins to one of the cowboys.

Ty dipped her and made like he was giving her a big kiss. Instead, he whispered, "If you were mine, I'd never let you go."

Once released from his embrace, she got a big hug from Louise and the same from Karen. They both made promises to visit her in New York.

Merry noticed Cait standing off to the side.

"Cait?" Merry bent down, held out her arms to the

girl and she came running. Her arms went around Merry's neck.

"I'm going to miss you so much, Caitie, but I promise to see you soon. And I'll call you, and you call me. Okay?"

"Okay, Merry."

"And I expect you to visit me. Remember how we talked about going shopping and seeing a show? I won't forget, and don't you forget either, sweetie."

"I won't forget."

Tears stung Merry's eyes. "I love you, Cait."

Cait had tears in her eyes, too. "I love you, Merry."

Merry gave her a kiss on both cheeks and on her forehead before she stood. Then she blew her another kiss.

Karen took Cait's hand and they slowly walked back to the house.

Only Buck remained.

It seemed as if they were strangers again.

She waited for another profession of love. She waited for him to ask her to stay, but he was as unreadable and as shut tight as a clam.

She looked back at the ranch house, etching it in memory. She wanted more than anything to stay right at the ranch that she had grown to love, the place that felt more like home to her than anywhere else.

All Buck had to do was ask her to stay.

She'd give it all up for him.

No. She'd give it all up for herself, too.

He tweaked his hat rim between his thumb and index finger. "Goodbye, Meredith *Bingham* Turner."

"Goodbye, Bucklin *Floyd* Porter." She didn't want him to see her cry.

Buck didn't say anything more. He just stared down at her. It was time for her to go.

She got into the gray rental, beeped goodbye and watched from her rearview mirror as Buck and the Rattlesnake Ranch disappeared from sight. Then she let her tears fall.

All she'd ever wanted was to have her own family and her own house that she could fuss with. Even more than that, she wanted Buck. She didn't want her own show in New York City if it meant coming home alone every night to an empty apartment. She wanted Buck and Cait…and Karen and Louise and Ty and Cookie and all the hands. She wanted the ranch house with its great history and its warm family vibrations. And she even wanted the desert.

Before, the desert had scared her, but now she thought that it was beautiful and wild and rugged and stubborn.

Just like a certain cowboy.

And her luck had held out. She'd never had a snake encounter.

She passed Dan heading back to the Rattlesnake, so she beeped and waved. She wondered what Buck's reaction would be when he saw his motorcycle again, and hoped he'd just accept it and not let his ego overwhelm his good sense.

A fresh batch of tears blurred her vision, and she couldn't even see the road. She knew she had to pull over, mop up her face and get herself under control.

Taking a deep breath, she got out of the car and looked down the valley. The ranch looked like a tiny speck in the distance. Then she checked the area around her.

Okay, so she was still cautious about snakes and crawling things. But then she realized it was much more than that. This was the exact same spot where she'd first met Buck.

Then the burros arrived, just like before. "You must live around here," she said.

Merry wiped her tears and gave a small laugh as she reached to pet one. The other started nibbling on the hem of her blazer, but she shooed him away. "Not this time." One starting chewing on the back bumper. She laughed as they pushed her back against the car with their nose. "Get on with you."

When Buck walked back into the ranch house, all was quiet. Five pair of eyes stared at him: Ty's, Karen's, Louise's and Cait's, and the new kitten's.

"What?" he asked.

No one said anything. They just shook their heads. Then Cait said, "Go get her, Daddy."

"Cait? What did you say?"

"I love her and I want her to be my mommy." Cait got up from the couch and stood in front of him. Her head was bent so far back to look up at him that her pigtails were almost touching the floor. "Please bring her back. She likes you, too. She likes you a lot."

Karen, Louise and Ty sat staring, dumbfounded. He hadn't told them yet about what had happened in the barn.

But no one was more dumbfounded than he. Cait was speaking her mind.

He picked her up—she was still as light as he remembered—and didn't pull away. "I love Merry, too, and I don't want her to leave."

Cait tugged on the sleeves of his shirt. "Then go get her before she goes back to Boston."

"Another bossy woman in the house," Buck mumbled, but he was so happy that he could burst. "I'll bring her back. Don't go away, Cait. We have a lot of talking to do—you, me and Merry."

He gave her a kiss on the cheek, and she didn't shrug away. She was smiling at him!

"Go, brother," yelled Ty.

"Go," shouted Lou.

"I knew it would work," added Karen. "You both just needed a little time together."

When Buck stepped out on the porch, Dan was pulling up with the Panhead.

Buck found Merry laughing and petting the same burros that she'd been scared of several days ago. He rode up on the Panhead with a note stuffed in his shirt pocket—the message that Merry had given to Dan for him. It read, "Buck, follow your dream. Love always, Merry."

He cut the motor. "I don't want to say anything stupid. I spewed enough stupidity in the barn last night."

He reached into his pocket, pulled out her note and handed it to her. "You're my dream, Merry, and I'll follow you. If you want to live in New York City or

Boston or in Paris, I'll live there with you, because I can't live without you. I love you. Marry me."

She smiled, then shook her head. His heart sank. She was going to turn him down.

"I don't want to live in any of those places. I want to live right here with you—in the ranch house—the house that has been in your family for generations. I want to make our babies in the tree bed."

"I'll do my part." His heart beat wildly. "But what about New York?" He took off his hat, ran a hand through his hair, then plopped the hat back on. "I can't tie you down, and I don't want you to resent me."

"I could never resent you, Buck. My heart isn't in New York or Boston. My heart is right here. I'd like to work on some Southwestern cookbooks, and I can do that from the ranch."

Buck got off the motorcycle and walked toward Merry, the movement scaring the burros, who moved down the road.

"What about your parents? They aren't going to like the fact that you're marrying a cowboy." He shrugged. "Actually, I'm worse than public TV, aren't I?"

"Perhaps." She laughed. "I'm following my dreams, too, Buck. And if they can't accept you…well, that's their problem."

Merry stood straight and her voice was confident. "And, anyway, if I can handle wild burros, I can handle my parents."

"You have a point there." He couldn't stop smiling.

"How many?" she asked.

"How many…what?"

Merry reached for her purse in the front seat and pulled out a pen and her notebook. She flipped to a clean page, and her pen hovered over it. "How many kids?"

"However many we're blessed with."

"Will you make their home as loving as yours was when you were a kid?"

"Yes. Absolutely. Of course," he assured her.

"Another thing. I don't want the ranch to be a dude ranch." She tried to hold back a smile. "I hope you don't mind."

"I'm terribly disappointed," he said, clutching his heart. "Are you sure that's not negotiable?"

"Not negotiable at all. I don't want a bunch of people interrupting us in the tree bed."

He whistled. "No problem. I'll see to it personally."

She pretended to write in her notebook. "Speaking of people, your brother and sisters are welcome at any time, but they need to follow their own dreams…which leads to our big problem—my money. When we get married, it'll belong to both of us. And I want you to use it to buy out your sisters and brother."

"Merry, I—"

"It's not negotiable. Karen can start her own business. Lou can start up her law office, and Ty…well, he can do whatever he wants to do."

Buck looked a little sheepish. "Karen said that marriage is like a merger. And that I can give you things that money can't buy, and vice versa."

"What do you think I've been trying to tell you all along?" She looked up to the sky and raised her hands. "What made that finally sink in?"

"The thought of losing you." He cupped her cheek and saw the joy in her eyes. His chest tightened and he hugged her tight to him. "Karen thinks that you're successful at what you do because you like being a homemaker, to a great extent." Buck looked off at Lizard Rock. "I think she was only half right, Merry."

"What do you think?"

"I think you create your own happy home with every meal you make and with every place you decorate because you didn't have a happy home when you were a child."

Damn, if the cowboy wasn't right.

"Buck, will you shut up and kiss me?"

"But we're in a public place." He pointed to the burros grazing at the side of the road. "Any one of those could be a reporter in a burro suit."

She pushed him away, laughing. "The hell with the tabloids. I just don't care anymore. I love you, Bucklin Floyd Porter, and I don't care who knows it."

He took off his hat and tossed it. "Yee-haw!" He lifted her off the ground and twirled in a circle.

She was dizzy with happiness. He set her down but held her close again and rubbed her back. "Thanks for the bike, too."

"I just couldn't let you sell it. Your grandfather gave it to you."

"And thanks for giving Cait back to me. She about yelled at me to go and bring you back. She wants you to be her mother."

"Oh, Buck." Tears of joy flooded her eyes.

"It's because of you, you know. You reached my little girl."

He took her into his arms. He could feel her heart beating next to his. Thank goodness he had come to his senses.

She looked up at him, her eyes full of mischief. "And I might as well tell you that I bought all of Olan Gunderson's bulls. I told him that I was buying them for Karen as a get-well gift instead of a flower arrangement. I don't think he believed me, but he'll be delivering your sperm donors this afternoon."

Buck stiffened.

"You've come a long way, Buck. Please don't let your pride get in the way of our happiness. I can't change the fact that I have money, so let's just use it to make *both* our dreams come true."

Buck wasn't easy to convince, but she could see that he was trying like hell.

He looked out over the valley as if he were searching for answers on the horizon.

"Okay, you've convinced me," he finally said. "But how about one stipulation? I'd like to pay off the debt on the ranch myself. If the gallery sale comes up short, I'll keep on making furniture."

"If it'll make you feel better, it's a deal. And I'd like you to make me a bookcase and a desk when you get a chance. I'll share your office."

"Deal," Buck echoed. "Now, do you think we should have Louise draw everything up, nice and legal, or should I have my people talk to your people?" He cupped his hands around his mouth and shouted to the burros, "Is there a notary in the crowd?"

She chuckled. "Our verbal agreement is binding as

far as I'm concerned. But we could seal the deal with a kiss."

"Are we done with negotiations now?" he asked, then cupped his hands around his mouth and shouted to the burros, "Is there a notary in the crowd?"

She looked into his eyes and smiled. "I think we're done."

"Well, I have just one more thing," he said, nibbling on her ear and her neck.

"What's that?" She could barely speak.

He took the notebook and pen from her hand. He wrote something and handed it back to her.

She read his note, put her arms around his waist and kissed the stuffing out of him. "That's sealing the deal with more than a kiss."

"I drive a hard bargain." His blood heated up and sweat broke out on his upper lip when he thought of what he'd written. "Damn, I'm hot."

"It's the desert," Merry said.

"Not this time. It's you." He handed her a helmet. "I'll send a couple of the boys back for the car." Buck took the hand of the woman he was going to marry.

"I love you, Merry."

Buck's lips met hers, and Merry knew that she had found what she'd been looking for all her life.

* * * * *

*Experience entertaining women's fiction about
rediscovery and reconnection—warm, compelling
stories that are relevant
for every woman who has wondered
"What's next?" in their lives.
After all, there's the life you planned.
And there's what comes next.*

*Turn the page for a sneak preview
of a new book from Harlequin NEXT.*

*CONFESSIONS OF A NOT-SO-DEAD LIBIDO
by Peggy Webb*

*On sale November 2006,
wherever books are sold.*

My husband could see beauty in a mud puddle. Literally. "Look at that, Louise," he'd say after a heavy spring rain. "Have you ever seen so many amazing colors in mud?"

I'd look and see nothing except brown, but he'd pick up a stick and swirl the mud till the colors of the earth emerged, and all of a sudden I'd see the world through his eyes—extraordinary instead of mundane.

Roy was my mirror to life. Four years ago when he died, it cracked wide open, and I've been living a smashed-up, sleepwalking life ever since.

If he were here on this balmy August night I'd be sailing with him instead of baking cheese straws in preparation for Tuesday-night quilting club with Patsy. I'd be striving for sex appeal in Bermuda shorts and bare-toed sandals instead of opting for comfort in walking shoes and a twill skirt with enough elastic around the waist to make allowances for two helpings of lemon-cream pie.

Not that I mind Patsy. Just the opposite. I love her. She's the only person besides Roy who creates wonder wherever she goes. (She creates mayhem, too, but we won't get into that.) She's my mirror now, as well as my compass.

Of course, I have my daughter, Diana, but I refuse to be the kind of mother who defines herself through her children. Besides, she has her own life now, a husband and a baby on the way.

I slide the last cheese straws into the oven and then go into my office and open e-mail.

From: "Miss Sass" <patsyleslie@hotmail.com>
To: "The Lady" <louisejernigan@yahoo.com>
Sent: Tuesday, August 15, 6:00 PM
Subject: Dangerous Tonight
Hey Lady,
I'm feeling dangerous tonight. Hot to trot, if you know what I mean. Or can you even remember? ? Look out, bridge club, here I come. I'm liable to end up dancing on the tables instead of bidding three spades. Whose turn is it to drive, anyhow? Mine or thine?

XOXOX
Patsy
P.S. Lord, how did we end up in a club with no men?

This e-mail is typical "Patsy." She's the only person I know who makes me laugh all the time. I guess that's why I e-mail her about ten times a day. She lives right next door, but e-mail satisfies my urge to be instantly and constantly in touch with her without having to interrupt the flow of my life. Sometimes we even save the good stuff for e-mail.

From: "The Lady" <louisejernigan@yahoo.com>
To: "Miss Sass" <patsyleslie@hotmail.com>
Sent: Tuesday, August 15, 6:10 PM
Subject: Re: Dangerous Tonight

So, what else is new, Miss Sass? You're always dangerous. If you had a weapon, you'd be lethal.
Hugs,
Louise
P.S. What's this about men? I thought you said your libido was dead?

I press Send then wait. Her reply is almost instantaneous.

From: "Miss Sass" <patsyleslie@hotmail.com>
To: "The Lady" <louisejernigan@yahoo.com>

Sent: Tuesday, August 15, 6:12 PM
Subject: Re: Dangerous Tonight
Ha! If I had a *brain* I'd be lethal.
And I said my libido was in hibernation, not DEAD!
Jeez, Louise!!!!!
P

Patsy loves to have the last word, so I shut off my computer.

* * * * *

Want to find out what happens to their friendship when Patsy and Louise both find the perfect man?

Don't miss
CONFESSIONS OF A NOT-SO-DEAD LIBIDO
by Peggy Webb,

coming to Harlequin NEXT
in November 2006.

HARLEQUIN®

NeXt™

Entertaining women's fiction for every woman who has wondered "what's next?" in her life.

HNCOUPUS

 HARLEQUIN®

NeXT™

**Entertaining women's fiction
for every woman who has
wondered "what's next?"
in her life.**

Receive $1.⁰⁰ off

any Harlequin NEXT™ novel.

Coupon expires March 31, 2007.
Redeemable at participating retail outlets
in Canada only. Limit one coupon per customer.

52607178

HNCOUPCDN

nocturne™

USA TODAY bestselling author

MAUREEN CHILD

ETERNALLY

He was a guardian. An immortal fighter of evil,
out to destroy a demon, and she was his next
target. He knew joining with her would make
him strong enough to defeat any demon.
But the cost might be losing the woman
who was his true salvation.

On sale November, wherever books are sold.

This holiday season, cozy up with

HARLEQUIN® *Romance*

*In November
we're proud to present*

JUDY CHRISTENBERRY
Her Christmas Wedding Wish

A beautiful story of love and family found.

And

LINDA GOODNIGHT
Married Under The Mistletoe

Don't miss this installment of

The Brides of Bella Lucia

From the Heart. For the Heart.

HRXMAS06

COMING NEXT MONTH

SSECNM1006